FLY ME TO THE MOON

FLY ME TO THE MOON

SYLVIA STRYKER
SPACE CASE #1

DIANE VALLERE

 POLYESTER PRESS BOOKS | Los Angeles, CA

Copyright Page

FLY ME TO THE MOON
Sylvia Stryker Space Case #1
A Polyester Press Publication

Second edition.

First published December 2017 as MURDER ON MOON TREK 1. Original ISBN 9781939197405

Copyright © 2018, 2017 Diane Vallere

Print edition ISBN: 9781939197542

DEDICATION

To Jordaina Sydney Robinson

for her friendship, enthusiasm, determination,

and rhino hide.

ACKNOWLEDGMENTS

This book would not exist if not for a childhood introduction to *Star Trek* and more recent exposure to the vast catalog of work created by Gerry and Sylvia Anderson. Thank you, Eva Hartmann with Your Fiction Editor, for helping me refine the story I set out to tell. Thanks, too, to the subscribers to The Weekly DiVa who answered my call for help to name the captain of the Moon Unit, most notably Sandy Ingram, Faye Trammel, Katherine Munro, and Connie Edwards, from whose suggestions I landed a proper name, and to The Polyester Posse, for your efforts on my behalf. And to Josh Hickman, who rose to the challenge of "I want to watch space movies" and sought out the most obscure titles that could be found on the internet. You are the dilithium crystal that keeps my warp (warped?) drive functioning.

MOON UNIT CREW AND PASSENGER MANIFEST

(RESULTS OF PRELIMINARY BACKGROUND CHECK)

Beryn: Communication director. Martian. Little. Green. Male.

Cat: robot cat assembled and customized by self-taught future security expert Sylvia Stryker. Performs various computer functions in addition to acting like a cat.

Daila Teron: Original uniform lieutenant. Unfortunate illness days before departure created last-minute job opening on Moon Unit 5.

Dakkar Teron: Second navigator. Victim. Wearing red shirt when found.

Doc Edison: Head of Medi-Bay. Cranky.

Jack Stryker: Sylvia's dad. Former owner of dry ice mine. Currently serving life sentence in Federation Council prison. From Plunia. Married to human. Let's not talk about him.

Neptune: Head of security on Moon Unit 5. Large, intimidating dude. Background: classified and unhackable. Darn!

Pika: pink Gremlon alien who has snuck on board the ship. Possible troublemaker.

Purser Frank: Responsible for passenger-facing activities. Oversees movement of supplies on board the spaceship.

Space Pirates: Bad dudes who do bad things.

Sylvia Stryker: space academy dropout. Half Plunian and half human. Has lavender skin. Grew up on dry ice farm. Difficulty breathing unregulated air without bubble helmet. Acting uniform lieutenant aboard Moon Unit 5. ~~Overqualified.~~

Thaddeus Swift: Captain of Moon Unit 5. Friend of Neptune. Has bright red hair.

Uma Tolst: Entertainment Director aboard Moon Unit 5. Reports to Purser Frank. Manages The Space Bar and Ion 54.

Vaan Marshall: Youngest member of Federation Council. Sylvia's first love. From dwarf planet Plunia. Is purple.

Yeoman D'Nar: Sylvia's direct boss. In charge of uniform ward. Wears pearly blue lipstick and nail polish. Has unhealthy obsession with identifying wardrobe infractions.

Zeke Champion: Son of space ship repairman. Expert on hacking and space drone technology.

1: NEPTUNE

When Moon Unit 5 kicked off its inaugural trip from my home planet of Plunia, I expected the uniform closet to be stuffed to capacity. I just hadn't expected it to be stuffed with a body. But here we were, light years from the space station where we'd departed, and instead of a closet of freshly laundered uniforms, I had a dead man. No matter how thoroughly I'd planned for today, I never could have planned for this.

Maybe he wasn't dead. Maybe he was tired. Maybe he'd had a late night partying before today's departure and crawled into my uniform closet to take a nap.

As unlikely as that explanation was, I wasn't yet willing to accept the more probable reality. I knelt next to him and checked for a pulse on the side of his neck. His skin was cold to the touch, which was either due to his not-alive state or the twenty-degree difference between earthling temperatures (his) and Plunian temperatures (mine). In this case, it was both. No pulse, no breathing. A Code Blue.

Moon Unit Corporation ran a fleet of cruise spaceships whose mission was to provide relaxing getaways to one of our galaxy's moons. Ever since I'd learned they were reopening after years of inactivity, I'd fantasized about working for them. The fact that I'd hacked my records into their system was a minor technicality. My job was to manage the uniforms during the moon trek, and as long as I did my job and avoided ship security, my fantasy would become a reality. But this was bigger than managing uniforms. Regardless of the risks to me, I had to contact the bridge.

I could send a general message over the staff communication network. I stepped away from the pile of spilled uniforms and shifted to the computer that sat above the console in the middle of the room. It was standard issue, a flat black folio with colorful buttons and a low-definition screen. Only the top members of the ship and paying passengers were given high-def equipment. For the rest of us, it was the bare minimum, Moon Unit Corporation's way of making sure distractions didn't surround us. To the right side of the computer was a clear plastic dome that protected a shiny red button that, despite learning about during emergency protocol training, I'd hoped never to have to use.

This was a button message.

I flipped the dome up and pressed the button. "Uniform Ward to the bridge. Lieutenant Sylvia Stryker reporting. There's a situation in my ward."

"What kind of situation?" asked a female voice. It sounded like my immediate supervisor, Yeoman D'Nar. There was no official reason for her to be on the bridge during departure, but senior officers of the ship were given an open invitation to witness the launch with Captain Swift. D'Nar was exactly the type to insert herself where she wasn't wanted.

"I'm pretty sure it's a Code Blue." Pretty sure? I was completely sure. There was no doubt I was looking at a Code Blue.

"Don't be reckless. A Code Blue is serious. I think you made a mistake."

I bristled at her accusation but kept my voice in check. "It's not a mistake. I memorized the codes last night."

"I don't think you have a Code Blue. Check the BOP and report in as applicable."

The BOP—Book of Protocols—was a 237-page manual that outlined the proper method for handling everything from hydrating vacuum-packed meals to subordination expectations between low-level officers and high-ranking ones. Every ship in the galaxy had a BOP. Crew members were expected to know the rules and regulations of the ship, but the BOP existed as a backup when something unexpected happened.

I picked up a small hand mirror from the nearby uniform alterations station and held it in front of the officer's mouth. No condensation.

Code Blue, alright.

I hadn't been lying about having memorized the list of codes from the BOP. I'd bought a used copy of an old Book of Protocols from the black market and studied it from cover to cover. No doubt it was outdated. The Moon Units 1-3 had had their share of trouble, and the problems with the Moon Unit 4 were still classified, but I had to start somewhere.

I flipped through the pages of the Moon Unit 5 BOP, looking for an updated list of warning codes. Because my knowledge had come from the old BOP, I'd created a finding tool: a cross-reference of everything in the old manual and where to find it in the new one. I'd also had a copy of the BOP made and organized it the way I would if

I were in charge of ship security.

Someday, I would be. When people stopped judging me by what my dad had done before they arrested him and took him away.

But today wasn't someday, and even though the bridge blew off my call, I still had a problem that had nothing to do with uniform management.

I studied the deceased officer. Who was he? A quick assessment of his uniform indicated his position and rank: red shirt, two bands circling his cuff, standard issue black pants, and gravity boots. Second navigation officer of Moon Unit 5.

There were no visible wounds to indicate how he'd died. He wasn't wearing an air purification helmet like I was, so I disconnected my inhalation tube from the oxygen tank under my uniform, held the tube in front of his mouth, and sniffed. Cherries and menthol. I reconnected the tube and then put my hand under his chin and opened his mouth wide. His tongue had a stripe of bright red down the middle like he'd been sucking on a throat lozenge. It was common practice among crew members during takeoff because frequent swallowing kept ears from plugging up.

"What are you doing?" said a voice behind me. I turned my head and bumped my protective fiberglass bubble helmet on the closet door. My helmet bounced off the surface. I blinked a few times and then looked up.

Uh-oh.

Even if I'd been face to face with the man in the uniform ward, he would have towered over me. He had a bald head and dark, pointed eyebrows that shielded dark eyes. Long, straight nose and lips that were drawn in a line and turned down on the sides. His arms crossed in front of his body, and his biceps bulged below the hem of the short sleeves of his dark blue jumpsuit.

My mind flashed over a series of facts and images I'd memorized before my official first day, and I reached one conclusion. This man was from the maintenance crew. My know-it-all boss must have told him I called in the wrong code and sent him here to clean up whatever mess I'd caused.

"I'm Sylvia Stryker. I spoke with Yeoman D'Nar about a Code Blue. Did she send you?"

He looked over my shoulder at the body. "Move," he said.

I stood quickly. The action triggered a bout of vertigo. I put my hand on my counter just behind where I'd left the open Book of Protocols. Yikes! If this guy saw that I'd torn apart and rearranged the protocol manual, he'd report me to ship security without a second thought. I moved a few inches to the left and turned around to block his view of the counter.

"They must have notified you. You're with maintenance, right?"

His expression didn't change. "I haven't heard anything about a Code Blue."

"Oh." I looked over my shoulder to where I'd moved the body. "Maybe the bridge was busy with takeoff."

Unlike my uniform, the muscular man's didn't have the Moon Unit insignia—a silver number 5 surrounded by circles on their axis like the rings around Saturn, all contained in an orange patch edged in black thread. It was the same insignia on my ID card and woven into the carpet in the employee lounge and on the cover of the BOP and every single uniform in the inventory closet. But it wasn't on him.

Still, the deceased officer deserved to be in a more honorable location than the inventory closet and I needed help moving him. But since there was the tiniest chance that ship security would uncover the fact that I hadn't indeed been hired through proper channels and might be viewed as a stowaway on board the ship, I'd planned to lay low until we'd cleared the breakaway point in our moon trek. Maybe Yeoman D'Nar's lack of urgency was a blessing in disguise.

"He's dead," I said.

"How?"

"I don't know. He was inside the uniform closet when I got here. I checked for a pulse but couldn't find it."

"You need to notify the bridge."

"Well, duh," I said. "I probably know the ship protocols better than you do. I contacted the bridge and told Yeoman D'Nar I had a Code Blue, but she didn't believe me." I looked at the body over the large man's shoulder. "Can you help me move him? I have to prep for departure, and I can't do that while he's blocking my inventory."

The man's back was to me, but he turned his head to the side so I could see his profile. His eyebrow raised again. He slipped his arms under the officer's neck and knees and then stood up and lifted him like he was lifting a bag of potatoes. Plunia was filled with potato farms, and when I wasn't working in the ice mines with my mom, I'd often played in the potato fields. I was pretty sure Plunian potatoes weighed a lot less than the second nav officer.

The maintenance man set the body on the reclining bench alongside the inside wall of the uniform ward. He draped a dressing gown over him, covering his face and red shirt. The dressing gown was only so long, though, so the officer's bottom half still showed.

"Your ward is off limits," the maintenance man said.

"No!" I said. "I mean, this is my job on the ship. I expect today to be slow because everybody is probably wearing their best uniform, but still, if I don't open the uniform ward, the crew will ask questions."

"Do you have something to hide?" he asked.

I crossed my arms over my magenta uniform. "You ask a lot of questions for a janitor."

He seemed surprised, and then his lips pressed together, and the corners of his mouth turned up. "Why do you think I'm the janitor?"

"I don't recognize your uniform, and I know all the different ones on the ship. The only people on the ship wearing uniforms that don't come from my ward are the janitorial crew."

The cabin doors swished open and a man in gray walked in. "Neptune, Captain Swift is waiting for you in engineering. He says the crack isn't sealed."

"Neptune?" I asked. I looked back and forth between the new guy and the one who'd been asking all the questions. "I thought Neptune was the head of Moon Unit security division?"

"I am," the original man said.

Oh, no. I'd heard about Neptune. He was the one person I'd been hoping to avoid.

2: THE MEDICAL CREW

My lavender skin flushed hot, and I felt like my whole body was on fire. Until the ship's air pressure had stabilized, I needed to wear my helmet. Air must have leaked into it when I'd hit it on the closet, and now my equilibrium was completely off.

Why would someone so high up in the company be here on the ship? I wanted to remind Mr. Neptune that the captain needed him in the engineering quadrant, but considering the precarious nature of my presence on the ship in the first place, I chose to keep my mouth shut and play it cool. Nobody said anything else for an uncomfortable couple of seconds.

"Where's the uniform lieutenant?" Neptune asked.

"I'm the uniform lieutenant."

"No, you're not. Daila Teron is. Where is she?"

"She—she was sick and couldn't make the launch. I'm

her replacement." He studied me for an uncomfortable couple of seconds. "It was a last-minute thing," I added.

Neptune nodded as if he accepted my explanation. "I'll have the medical team come to collect the body."

"Wait," I said. "Who is he? What's his story?" I pointed at the body.

"He was the second navigation officer, just like you said."

"I know his rank. What's his name?"

"It doesn't matter."

"Yes, it does. He was a person."

"Crew members check our identities at the door when we board a ship."

"He was the second navigation officer. A member of the crew. He was a colleague."

He cut me off. "Call the bridge and tell them I confirmed your Code Blue." He turned to leave but stopped by the door. "His name was Dakkar," he said over his shoulder. Before I could ask any more questions, he left.

As soon as the men were out of my ward, I untwisted the controls on the side of my helmet and pulled it off my head. Cool air rushed at my skin. I dropped onto the end of the bench next to the dead officer—Lt. Dakkar, I repeated to myself—and closed my eyes. From the moment I'd discovered his body, I'd relied on my unemotional Plunian side to manage the circumstances, but now my earthling emotions overtook me.

My temperature was dangerously high, and if I couldn't cool down, I'd pass out. Plunians were not dissimilar to earthlings, except for one glaring difference: our skin was purple and ran about twenty degrees hotter than theirs. My mom was from Earth, but when it came to being judged by the color of my skin, there was no sense trying to hide my lineage. Purple is purple.

But that wasn't the problem. When the medical crew took me to the medical ward, they'd run enough tests to find out I had failed the entrance physical. After that, I'd be dropped off at the nearest space station. At least once we were past the breakaway point, they'd have to keep me on the ship until after the moon trek was over.

I reached up and picked at the seam of my uniform until I found a loose thread by the sleeve and then played with the seam until my fingers poked through. I was still burning up and needed to get air onto the surface of my skin. I tore the sleeves off and tossed them under the bench. I had another uniform in my quarters, and I could repair this one in my spare time. That was the problem with being part Plunian. I had wild swings in body temperature. My helmet helped, but it was against regulation, and I'd expected to ditch it as soon as I could. The body in the uniform closet had thrown me off.

Speaking of the body, I had been given a direct order from Neptune. I went back to the call button and radioed the bridge. "Uniform Ward to the Bridge, Sylvia Stryker reporting."

"This is the bridge," answered a computerized voice.

"I have a Code Blue. I've checked the BOP and—"

"Standby. Medi-Bay personnel will be there to collect the corpse in a moment. Over."

I recorded the call into my journal. Even though it had seemed way more likely that I'd take over the family business from my mom when she was ready to retire than ever work on a space ship, here I was. No matter what happened, I wanted to remember and document every single second of this experience so I could tell her all about it when I got home. It was just my luck that things had started out like this.

"Can you believe this?" I asked Lt. Dakkar's body. "Of all the people who could have walked into the uniform ward before we hit the breakaway point, I get the head of Moon Unit security. And what's he doing walking around in coveralls? Nobody's going to know he's security section if he's dressed like that."

Head smack. Of *course*, he was in coveralls and not a

uniform. Security wouldn't want to advertise their presence, especially not after what happened to the previous Moon Units. I'd read something about this somewhere.

I pulled my finding tool out of my personal belongings and cross-referenced the information back to the BOP in my center console. I found what I was looking for in a footnote on the page about the first trip made by a new Moon Unit.

Until the ship is cleared for departure and has passed the breakaway point into the galaxy, security personnel will remain in utility gear. Regulation uniforms are required for all other ship crew at all times. Additionally, throughout the moon trek, security is not to rely on any of the ship's wards for supplies. They are beholden to the safety of the ship only.

In doing my research on Moon Unit 5, I'd learned that in the past, security had developed loose loyalties to different departments and neglected others, and that had been the downfall of Moon Units 1-3. The truth about what had happened to Moon Unit 4 was kept tightly under wraps and remained a mystery despite how often I hacked into their chat room to read their security logs.

It was the physical that tripped me up, and all because my dad was from Plunia so my biological makeup came with a few challenges. Nothing I hadn't figured out how to handle by now.

The ward doors slid open, and a medical crew stepped inside. Doctor Edison, the ship's resident physician, led the team. Behind him was a pretty woman in a blue uniform that matched his own, followed by two men in standard gray. Gray was for flex crew members, trained to manage a variety of positions on the flight. Blue was for the medical staff (the uniform colors corresponded to their related codes, Code Blue meant medical, and the medical team wore blue.) He glanced my way, and I pointed to the body under the dressing gown. "The body is under there," I said. "He's the second navigation officer. Neptune confirmed his condition."

Doc pulled the dressing gown back from the body and ran a couple of standard tests. A series of whirs and buzzes and beeps sounded while his nurse assisted. After a few minutes, Doc stood up, capped the end of the nozzle that he'd used to take a sample of the inside of the officer's cheek, and handed it to the woman. Doc turned to me.

"What did Neptune tell you about him?"

"He didn't say anything. Neptune didn't even want to tell me his name."

"Why did you want to know his name?" Doc looked

suspicious.

"He was one of us. It seems right."

"Neptune was following protocol. Who told you he was the second navigation officer?"

"I'm in charge of uniforms. This officer is wearing a red shirt, and red shirts go with ship navigation. There's are two black bands around his left cuff, so he was second in command, not first. And the ship was able to depart from the space station, so he couldn't have been part of the main crew or they would have noticed he was missing from his post."

"Neptune didn't tell you any of that?" he asked.

"No. Neptune didn't say much of anything." As I stood in front of the doc and his assistant, I became aware that they were staring at my bare purple arms. I wrapped my arms around my body, but there was no covering the exposed flesh.

"You appear flushed. Are you feeling okay?" He stepped toward me and lifted his vital signs scanner.

"I'm fine," I said, stepping backward and out of range. "I was shaken up when I found the body and got a little warm."

Doc looked from my arms to my face. "What's your name?"

"Sylvia Stryker. Second Lieutenant."

"Stryker." He thought for a moment. "Come to the medical ward after your shift ends. I'd like to give you a physical."

Alarm bells sounded in my head. "I thought all of our physicals were conducted before departure," I said, carefully avoiding the truth about my own results.

"Lieutenant Stryker, you've been in contact with a dead man. I won't know what killed him until I give him a complete workup. You don't look all that hot yourself. It's my duty to make sure the crew stays healthy."

I wished I knew more about Lt. Dakkar, his background or his reason for being in the uniform ward. I wished I knew whether or not it was possible to catch something from a corpse. It was too late for that now.

"Every person on this ship has had a physical to clear them. I doubt he was sick, but I'm going to check his records and see what I can find out from an autopsy. In the meantime, I would request that you not mention this to the ship's guests. The captain has made it clear that a lot is riding on the success of Moon Unit 5, and the last thing we need is to create a panic. Do you hear what I'm saying, Lt. Stryker?" Doc Edison asked. "Until we know more, the details surrounding this man's death are not to be discussed."

"Of course. Confidentiality is understood."

The men in gray moved the body from my bench to a cart. They left the dressing gown over his face but draped him with a black blanket that covered the rest of him. The doors swished open, and the team departed as efficiently as they'd arrived. As soon as the doors swished shut behind them, I packed up my finding tool and put the BOP back onto the cabinet shelf where it was routinely stored. I reset the call button and locked the plastic dome into place on top of it, and then turned my attention back to the inventory closet. Previously neat stacks of uniforms sorted by size and color had been knocked out of place when the body had fallen out and were now in messy heaps on the floor.

"That's just great," I said. "Maybe I should have said I was a stowaway. At least that way I could avoid the humiliation of the physical and I wouldn't have to refold all these uniforms." I kicked the pile in front of me, and the stack fell over. "This whole thing was a huge mistake. I should have just stayed on Plunia and mined ice with my mom."

I scooped a pile of uniforms from the floor to the cabinet and scanned the room for a surface to use for folding. Just getting this inventory back into organization was going to take the better part of the day. "Stupid Sylvia," I muttered to myself. "This is your punishment for thinking you could get away with sneaking on board the ship. Sooner or later somebody's going to find out you're not supposed to be here."

I heard a noise behind the open cabinet door. Slowly, the door swung toward me, exposing a skinny pink alien girl who peeked out from behind it. She grinned at me in a manner so friendly that if she was a threat, I was the queen of the galaxy. She held both hands up in front of her. Her palms were dirty, as was the skin around her mouth. She looked like she'd picked a Plunian potato straight out of the ground and eaten it, dirt and all.

"I won't turn you in. I promise," she said. "But I do want to know how you managed to make it look like you belong here."

"Why?"

"Because you're like me! I mean, I'm like you! I mean, I'm a stowaway too."

3: PIKA THE STOWAWAY

Before I could say anything to the grinning alien girl in front of me, I heard the ward doors slide open. When I spun around, I was facing my boss.

Yeoman D'Nar was a tall, thin woman with golden blond hair, glowing skin, and legs that made her uniform barely the acceptable length without requiring alterations. She was only about five years older than I was, which meant she graduated from the space academy before I'd entered, but her legend was still fresh in the halls. She'd accomplished a lot in a short amount of time, and while it would have been easy to attribute her success to her looks, that very thought went against everything I wanted to believe regarding equal opportunity. I'd told myself she was the closest thing I'd have to a role model on the ship, but now that we were face to face, I could tell both her glacial attitude and penchant for pearly blue nail polish would be problematic when it came to finding commonalities between us.

"Lt. Stryker, you are in violation of the uniform code. I can't believe you would commit an infraction this soon in the moon trek. Do you know what would happen if one of our passengers saw you like that?"

"Like what?"

"Like that, all purple arms and perky breasts. The Moon Unit is a family ship. It's a good thing the doctor reported you to me. If you went out of this ward like that, Captain Swift would have to be notified."

We must have passed the breakaway point. The temperature in the uniform ward had dropped, and so had my body heat. I glanced around the room, looking for Pika. Surely the presence of a stowaway on board would be a bigger issue than my wardrobe infraction?

"Yeoman, did you see someone when you came in? Someone pink?"

"Don't try to distract me. You were hired aboard this ship to perform a simple task. Manage the uniforms for the crew. I'm both insulted and disappointed that on our first day of travel you would make a mockery of your department."

"I'm not making a mockery of anything."

"And the condition of this ward is appalling." She

pointed at the piles of uniforms, her pointy blue fingernail jabbing at the air. "Get these uniforms off the floor and back into that closet. I'm going to have to declare this ward off limits until you are back to ship standard. And if anybody—anybody!—finds out about this, you are going to be held personally accountable. I know the space academy trained you better than this."

I tried to remember what information I'd put on the application that I'd uploaded into the ship's database when I first learned the original uniform lieutenant had broken her leg and wouldn't be able to make the moon trek, but I couldn't. Everything about me being on this ship was the culmination of a carefully thought out plan. The events of the day were far too random to fit neatly into my expected organization.

The press surrounding Moon Unit 5 had stressed how the ship would run like clockwork. That the crew had been trained to make the trip to Ganymede, the largest of the moons that orbited Jupiter, and back in seven days. Ganymede had once been covered in ice, but a team of renegade meteorologists determined to regulate the weather had found a way to harness the sun's heat and not only melt the ice, but establish a protective gaseous layer of oxygen around the moon, making it one of the galaxy's most desirable destinations.

The ship's publicity department had gone out of their way to overcome the criticism that had lingered after the trouble with the first four Moon Units. The corporation had been out of service for the past ten years, and nobody had expected them to start running again. And here we were less than twenty-four hours into our journey and I'd found a body, been charged with a wardrobe infraction, and discovered a stowaway.

It was a darn good thing I'd memorized the Book of Protocols.

"The BOP makes allowances for uniform modification based on extreme changes in temperature and emergency situations. I admit that I did not seek out approval first, but while assisting both ship security and the medical staff with the discovery and movement of a dead body here in my ward, my uniform tore. I modified the garment before it became more damaged and plan to repair it when my shift ends. I take full responsibility for my decision."

Yeoman D'Nar's eyes flashed. She seemed angrier about my very plausible (and true!) explanation than she'd been over the discovery of the infraction in the first place.

"Where are your sleeves?"

I pointed to the floor under the bench.

She crossed the room and picked up the fabric, studied the seams where I'd torn them from the body of my garment, and then crumbled them into a wad and set the ball of fabric on top of my cabinet. "I expect that uniform to be in pristine condition when you report for duty tomorrow. You are to go directly from your shift to your quarters and not leave for the rest of the night. That is non-negotiable. Do you understand?"

"Yes, Yeoman. I understand completely." I understood that she had just given me an acceptable reason not to go to the medical ward when my shift was over. Inside I smiled. To her, I forced my face into a serious expression to match her reprimand.

"Good. Now get this ward back up to standard and notify me when you're done." She spun on the heel of her gravity boots and left.

As soon as the doors swooshed shut behind her, I closed the closet door and faced Pika. She was still grinning. "You're not supposed to be on the ship. You're going to get in trouble. We're going to have fun!"

"Who are you?"

"I told you. I'm Pika!"

"*What* are you?"

"I'm a Gremlon. I hitchhiked from Colony 7 to the space station and snuck on board. Where did you come

32

from?"

There was something joyful and likable about Pika, but as soon as she said she was a Gremlon, I knew I had to be careful.

Gremlons were an alien race that mostly lived on Colony 7, not because space travel was all that hard to come by these days, but because their overwhelming sense of trickery was more important to them than loyalties. The Gremlon usually found employment in the entertainment industries. They were colorful and wild and exuberant. They were tons of fun to be around, and the more successful of them had found ways to parlay their wild side into performances that people paid to see. But because they had no sense of how far was too far, they often ended up in trouble. More than half of the prisoners in the Plunian jail system were Gremlons. Colony 7 was the one place where their trickery was the norm.

"I don't know what you think you heard, but you probably misunderstood me. It's been a stressful morning."

"Yes! Because you found a dead guy in your closet and then the giant made you hot and then the doc said he wants to probe you. Space probe! Watch out! And then the mean lady with the crabby face made fun of your outfit." Pika acted out everything she said, shifting from limp arms hanging by her sides to illustrate the dead officer to raising her arms above her head to represent Neptune, the giant. She scrunched up her face to imitate Yeoman D'Nar's angry expression. It was like watching a one-woman show. I didn't want to laugh, but I couldn't help myself. In thirty seconds, she'd captured the highlights (and lowlights) of my morning.

"What are you going to do? What are you going to do? What are you going to do?" She slapped the tips of her fingers against my forearm in a blur, not hurting me but causing a slight stinging sensation.

I stepped backward and held my hands up. "I'm here as the uniform lieutenant. I'm going to do my job."

"But you're not you're not you're not," she said.

"Why do you say everything three times?"

"Because it's funny!" She jumped out from behind the closet door and bounced back and forth from one foot to the other, making goofy gestures with her hands.

"It won't be funny if you make so much noise that they come in here and catch you."

"Us."

"You."

"Us."

"*You*. I have a cover story."

Her face fell and the small pointy ears atop her head

wilted slightly. *Don't be a fool, Sylvia*, I told myself. *It's an act.* But the longer she stayed sad, the more I needed to cheer her up again. "Fine. Help me get these uniforms folded and back into the closet. And here," I said, holding out an extra small gray general crew member uniform, "put this on so you don't stand out so much."

Her ears perked up, and she grinned again. I had a feeling Pika's "help" was going to be minimal.

I looked around the rest of the uniform ward. Now that the body was gone, the ward looked like I'd expected. Utilitarian-beige walls. Orange carpet. Locked emergency cabinet on the back wall next to a ten-key pad to gain access. Every ward on the Moon Unit held emergency equipment. Only first officers had the passcodes.

Pika pulled on the uniform and skipped in circles around the ward while I folded the inventory. Every once in a while, she stopped and put her hands on her hips.

"Where are you from?" she asked.

"Plunia."

Plunia had been "discovered" about three hundred years ago even though we'd been in existence far longer than that. Massive overpopulation of Earth, the third planet from the sun, had led to space exploration in the solar system. Soon enough, those explorers discovered that the planets that revolved around the sun were only a fraction of what existed in the universe.

When those explorers reported back that the Plunian atmosphere was similar to theirs, earthlings started moving in. No one had anticipated the newcomers, and there'd been a war. But the realities of how vast the universe really was, and how little everyone knew about it, forced odd partnerships. Earth was still out there, somewhere closer to the sun than was comfortable to me, but entire pockets of their scientific community had established labs on other planets. Medical breakthroughs came from collaborations between Uranians and Saturnians, and everyday checkups were conducted by a full body scan created by a former airline security agent who found work on a dwarf planet.

Pika considered my response. and then resumed skipping. A few minutes later, she stopped. "What are your parents?"

"Plunian and earthling."

She thought about that for a moment and skipped some more. Her questions were direct and seemed to come from a place of pure curiosity, and I found it easier to drop my guard and answer truthfully than try to come up with lies. I'd been so worried about accidentally letting someone learn I didn't belong that it felt good just to be honest.

"What's your mom do?" she asked, this time not bothering to stop skipping. I'd gotten most of the uniforms off the floor, and Pika's path was less obstructed.

"She's a dry ice miner." Ever since the advent of commercial space travel, scientists had been looking for ways to make the Kuiper belt livable. Ice mines on Plunia, Pluto, Mars, and Neptune helped solve the problem because they produced oxygen. Mills that purified the ozone made formerly uninhabitable planets habitable.

"What about your dad?"

"He's in jail."

"On Plunia?"

"No, on Colony 13."

Pika stopped skipping. Her eyes widened, and she looked scared. "What did he do? Uh-oh!" Before I could answer or react to her sudden change, she sprung across the room and wedged herself behind the closet door where she'd been when I first discovered her.

The doors swooshed open and Neptune entered. "Stryker," he said.

I whipped my head back around from where Pika was hiding to face the giant security guard. "Neptune. I mean Mr. Neptune. I mean, do you have a title?"

"It's just Neptune.

"Why isn't it Mr. or Commander or Sargent or Admiral? Detective? The doc called you Neptune. Why?"

"Never mind the doc. He doesn't like me." Well, that wasn't passive aggressive at *all*. "I need to ask you some follow-up questions about this morning."

"Okay," I said. I remained on the opposite side of my counter, with the structure acting as a protective barrier between us. Depending on the nature of Neptune's questions, I was toast. "Fire away."

He crossed his arms. I suspected he did that when he wanted to look more intimidating. It worked. The fabric of his shirt stretched across his massive chest. He was like a wall. Who was I kidding? If he wanted to get me from the other side of the cabinet, he probably could have reached over it and lifted me by the front of my magenta uniform. He was probably thinking that very thing, considering how his eyes were affixed on my uniform instead of my face.

Oh, crap.

I'd forgotten about my wardrobe infraction. I should have changed into a new uniform after Yeoman D'Nar left, but Pika had appeared out of nowhere and distracted me, and now I was half naked in front of the head of ship security. Perky, too.

Double crap!

"My sleeves got caught on the cabinet," I said. "I thought it was more important to stay here with Lt. Dakkar's body—"

"Don't use his name."

I hated the detached feeling of calling the deceased officer by his position, but Neptune outranked me and he'd given me a direct order.

"I thought it was more important to stay here with the body of the second nav officer than to go to my quarters to change."

"This is the uniform ward," he said. "You could have changed here."

A whole lot of people were content to point out the obvious. "It's a good thing I didn't. You would have walked in on me naked." Neptune's eyes went back to my chest. "I'll change when my shift is over."

"I'm afraid that's not going to be possible. You need to come with me."

"I can't. I'm on duty. And when I'm done I have to go straight to my quarters per Yeoman D'Nar." Neptune's forehead scrunched in confusion. I pointed to my arms. "To repair my uniform," I added.

"What you wear is no longer a problem. Sylvia Stryker, you're under arrest for impersonating a crew member of Moon Unit 5."

4: ARRESTED

I'd been careful from the moment I'd stepped foot on the ship. I didn't know how he knew. There was no point in arguing the point with him because it was the truth. Even if I *was* qualified to be on board. Even if I *had* studied at the space academy, continued with my education after I was forced to drop out, applied for a job like everybody else, and aced the entrance exams. I was more qualified to be a part of this ship's crew than almost anybody here.

Stupid Plunian blood. It was one more thing to blame my dad for.

I left the uniform closet wide open and joined Neptune by the door. He held a space gun, but it was pointed at the floor. The BOP dictated any time security had to manage a crew infraction, they were to have their weapon in hand. I looked at Neptune. "I know the BOP says you have to have your space gun out, but you won't have to use it on me."

"Standard procedure," he said.

"Fine." We walked side by side down the hall toward the elevator. The walls were smooth and white, and the carpet was an industrial orange weave. Even though Neptune was almost a foot taller than I was, I kept pace with him. I wasn't going to give him the satisfaction of prodding me to move faster.

We reached the end of the hall and unlocked the elevator. Two men in green shirts—food and nutrition crew—rounded the corner when we did. Neptune held up his hand and the men stopped. We got onto the elevator, and he inserted a key in the control panel. After he hit a series of colorful buttons, the elevator dropped straight down into the basement of the ship. My stomach didn't get the message, and, for a few seconds, I entertained a little bit of queasiness. I grabbed the railing and turned my back to Neptune while I made sure my breakfast was staying down. I felt, rather than saw, his movements behind me.

I didn't trust myself to let go of the railing or to look at him, so I glanced behind me and saw his space gun pointed at my back. "You can put that thing away. I'm not going to try anything. When we arrive at the subsection, I'll go directly to the holding cell. I just wasn't expecting the elevator to go so fast, that's all."

He relaxed his arm. The space gun once again pointed toward the floor. The elevator came to a stop as suddenly as it had started and my knees locked. The door swooshed open.

"Nice ride," I said. I turned left and followed the hallway to the large console that surrounded a master computer. To the right of the computer was a bare-bones holding cell. "You can't just lock me up," I said.

"Yes, I can. I know you aren't the uniform lieutenant."

"I told you, the original uniform lieutenant broke her leg and couldn't make the departure date. I was a last-minute replacement."

"No, you weren't." He turned behind him and pressed a couple of buttons on the computer. The screen lit up with the employee ID card for a brown haired, blue eyed woman who might have looked similar to me if her skin was purple. "Daila Teron was hired as the uniform lieutenant. But Daila isn't here, and you are. And judging from how you knew exactly where the holding cell was without me telling you, information that has been classified since the ship was designed, I'm going to assume you know more about the Moon Unit than most members of the crew. What I *don't* know is what you're planning to do with that knowledge."

I hadn't expected him to figure me out so quickly, and considering how long it had taken me to hack into the Moon Unit 5 database and replace Daila's information with my own, I wasn't in the mood to confess all my secrets. He thought he could figure me out? Let him.

"I didn't do anything wrong."

"You're on this ship illegally. You're impersonating the real uniform lieutenant. And you found a body this morning and didn't follow protocol."

"Hypothetically speaking, if I'm not a member of this ship's crew, then I'm not bound by protocol, so you don't get all three of those as points. But I *did* follow protocol, and if you look into it, you'll find out I'm telling you the truth." I walked into the cell and leaned against the far wall.

When they'd designed the Moon Unit spaceships, no expense or imagination had been spared. Passengers wanted to feel like they were part of a space adventure, and talented visionaries had responded to the call with fiberglass furniture, colorful Bakelite fixtures, and technologically advanced fabrics that could change their appearance through heat and light absorption. But down here in the unseen part of the ship, things were bleak. The floor and walls were coated with magnetic paint to block any communication, location, or radio signals that a prisoner might try to send, which made it slightly more challenging to move about properly since my uniform contained trace metals in the way of closures, zippers, and decorative trim. Either the supplier didn't anticipate the crew being locked up, or someone had a twisted sense of humor. I'd planned to customize my uniform and remove the metal trim when I had the chance. I just hadn't expected to get thrown in the clink mere hours after departure.

"I didn't lie about who I am." I reached into the pocket of my uniform and pulled out a square disc with a small chip embedded into it. "Run my credentials. I'm Sylvia Stryker. My family owns the ice mines on Plunia. We supply most of the ice that's used to create oxygen on other planets. You should be thanking me, not harassing me."

"Your dad is Jack Stryker?"

"Yes."

"That's what I thought."

Neptune pushed a thick red button on the wall outside the cell and beams of blue light appeared from the ceiling and the floor. Where they met in the middle, the light glowed orange.

Neptune took his finger off the button. "I trust you

know what will happen if you try to cross the beams."

"I don't feel like talking," I said. I crossed my arms and glared at him.

"Good. I was afraid you'd be a crier." For the first time since I'd met him, he smiled. His smile was genuine, but since it came at my expense, I didn't smile back.

Neptune attached his space gun to his belt and then watched me from the other side of the beams of light. I looked away from him, but after a few seconds, snuck a look back to see what he was doing. He hadn't moved and was still watching me.

"What happens now? I mean, you locked me up so you might think you have everything under control, but I had nothing to do with the death of the second navigation officer, so you still have a problem."

"I have two problems: the safety of everybody on this ship and a problem in engineering. You're not a problem. You can either cooperate or get dropped off at the space station. Your choice."

The head of security giving me a choice on whether I wanted to stay on the ship? This was great. This was *better* than great. This was so outside the realm of possibility that my mind spun with the sheer beauty of the moment, which was how I missed what he said next.

"You won't be sorry," I said.

His brow furrowed. "Did you hear me?"

"Most of it. Tell me again, just to make sure."

"There's somebody on this ship who intends to cause problems. I'm working on the assumption that if it were you, you would not have followed the BOP, so for now, I've decided you're less of a threat to the ship security than the person who is. I need to find that person, and I think we can help each other."

"I can help. Just tell me what you need."

"I pulled the passenger manifest. There were discrepancies. I can't do two things at once."

"You want me to take over ship security?"

"No. I need you to surveil the passengers and crew."

"But how will that help me?"

"I'm not interested in helping you. It's either that or get dumped on Colony 13 where you can share a cell with your father. Your choice."

5: LIGHT BULB MOMENT

"Fine," I mumbled.

"I'm glad we have an understanding." Neptune pushed a large red button on the wall, and the light beams disappeared. "Have a nice night, Stryker." He returned to the computer at the far end of the corridor.

Well, this was just great. I'd dreamed of this opportunity my whole life and I hadn't even been on the ship a full day before being found out.

I'd been so close. The change in temperature upstairs had indicated that we were well on our way to the moon. Captain Swift could choose to drop me off at one of the space stations along the way, but I doubted he would. An unscheduled stop would signify trouble, the last thing the publicity department would want. Discovering me must have been Neptune's worst nightmare.

That thought cheered me up a bit. At least until I

remembered that the moon trek was a seven-day long excursion and that if I wasn't going to be dropped off on the way to or from the moon, I was going to spend the next seven days either locked up or ratting on the people I'd hoped would become my friends.

I activated the elevator and returned to my quarters. I'd pictured a lot of potential scenarios for my first day on Moon Unit 5. Being arrested and placed in the temporary holding cell, even if only for a few minutes, was not one of them.

My room was small but perfect. The walls were glossy white with matte white circles on top. The doors were orange, as was the bed covering and the chair. I sat on the edge of my bed and removed my boots. The first thing I'd done after boarding the ship had been to unpack and get settled. I wanted to feel like this was my space *in* space. I spun around and stretched out on the bed, and then put my hands behind my head and stared up at the ceiling, studying the silver paint.

I read in the history books that it used to take four light years to go from Earth to its closest star. Thanks to technology, Moon Unit 5 could get us from Plunia to the moons of Saturn in a week—the perfect length of time for those in need of a vacation.

Space travel had originally been targeted toward the

rich, but it turned out the rich didn't quite know what to make of space pirates and all too soon, the novelty of being held up in ungoverned territories lost its luster. The second wave of entrepreneurs to tackle space travel made things interesting. They went with a price-it-low, sell-a-lot model, attracting the attention of the booming new generation. Now you'd be hard pressed to find someone over sixty on a spaceship. Traveling the galaxy had become *the* thing to do. At least that's what I'd thought before today.

I'd taken a huge risk to get here, left my mom alone with the ice mines, and for what? Ever since stepping foot onto the spaceship, things had gone from bad to worse. And it all started when I'd found Lt. Dakkar, the second navigator's body.

My reaction to it had been all wrong. Sure, I'd followed procedure, but almost to a fault. A man had died, and I'd reacted like a programmed robot, not like a person who discovered that a colleague had died. But here I was, with all the time in the world to think about what his death meant. And it did mean something. For the first time in a decade, a Moon Unit was in orbit with a ship full of passengers, and before the ship had even left the docking station, something tragic had happened.

I wondered what the second navigation officer had

been doing in the uniform ward. How had he gotten inside? And when? I'd been so eager for today to come that I'd been one of the first crew members on the ship. The only people who had been allowed to board before the general crew were the senior officers: captain, navigation, communications, engineering, medical, and security. The head of individual divisions, too, although I hadn't been able to get my hands on that list ahead of time. But if I operated with the knowledge I had, I could assume the second navigation officer had already been on the ship before the rest of the crew boarded.

Ship regulations stated that crew members were to arrive in uniform, so there shouldn't have been any reason for him, or anyone, to be where he was.

The questions swirling through my mind gave me anxious energy and I couldn't lay still. When my mind raced like this, I had to find a way to calm down. I sat up and pulled my boots back on, and then left my quarters.

I walked down the hall toward the observation deck and stared out a porthole at the vastness of space. The sky was a deep purply-black, dotted with gleaming stars and shifting meteors. The occasional spaceship passed us, far enough away that the only thing I could see were their lights. For a moment, I wondered about the crews on those other ships. Was there another person out there enjoying her first job on a spaceship? Was she flying through the galaxy peacefully or did she have her own set of problems?

That's what I had. Problems. I could solve problems. I needed to focus on one and solve it.

Just one. I could do that.

When I'd turned fourteen, I took a series of standardized tests like every other eight grader in the Plunian school system. But unlike every other eighth grader, I'd scored off the charts for math, science, and deductive reasoning. Fourteen marked the year when I went from being a nobody to a somebody.

The change in my academic status didn't help with my desire to fit in with others my age. If my family hadn't owned and operated one of the more successful dry ice mines on Plunia, I might not have had any friends at all. But when space pirates hijack the deliveries of dry ice to neighboring planets and your family is the only one who can step in and correct a mass oxygen shortage, you get a pass on being a little weird. Between that and the way I learned to fry Plunian potatoes with a tweaked thermostat wired to a refurbished radio coil and bucket of oil from the last olive crop, I avoided becoming a total social pariah.

It turned out I had a natural skill set for science. It's a

strange feeling to learn that you're really, really good at something other people don't understand. I couldn't explain it, but when I looked at a mechanical device, I could almost immediately map out the inner mechanisms and understand how it worked. I could take anything apart and put it back together. I knew how to make modifications so things would work better than they did before. I could fix things and change things and alter things to make life easier.

I would have been okay with that. I think. But one of my teachers took a special interest in me and arranged for me to take classes at the space academy. Twice a week, instead of English, I studied alongside students who were hoping to get into Federation Council. My parents took over the majority of the work in the mines and made it clear that my only focus was on my grades. And after a couple of classes, I felt like I fit in. Before long, I wanted to work at Federation Council too.

And then my dad was arrested, and everything changed.

I lost my scholarship and the very galactic government body I'd hoped to work for took temporary control of the family mines. They kept my mom working in a barely paid role while they investigated my dad. I dropped out of school and helped her survive the humiliation.

For the past ten years, I'd worked with her, secretly hating my Plunian dad and how his actions had destroyed us. I wasn't ever going to let greed make me do something that would hurt the people I loved.

After the investigation, ownership of the ice mines reverted to my mom. Being from Earth, she lacked the upper respiratory tolerance to work in the mines. I took over during the day and spent my nights working on gadgets to make her job easier. One day last year, the news reported that the council had approved the relaunch of the Moon Unit program. I hadn't even bothered to apply.

Turns out, it didn't matter. My mom had applied for me.

I'll never forget the day the confirmation packet arrived. "You're going to change the world, Sylvia, and you're not going to do it from Plunia."

"I'm not going to leave you alone to mine the ice," I'd said.

"I haven't mined the ice in ten years. I'm too old to be out there. The statute of limitations on punishing us for what your father did is over. This is your opportunity to get off this planet and make a life of your own."

A good daughter would have said she didn't want a

life of her own, or that her life was right there, taking over the family business. But I hadn't been able to say those words. The truth was, I'd thought of nothing but getting out of Plunia since the day they took my dad to space jail on Colony 13.

The Moon Unit staff called me for entrance exams. I passed them and aced my interview too. I'd started to believe that it was going to happen when the results of my physical came back.

Low tolerance of Nitrogen molecule limits physical endurance required of security personnel.

I'd never known there was a different chemical makeup to the air earthlings breathed. Plunia's air was 95% oxygen. It was part of what made us a healthy race that outlived the earthlings who had moved to our planet. But the Moon Unit wasn't designed for Plunians. It was staffed almost entirely of nomadic earthlings who were looking for adventure. Which meant the air was 78% nitrogen and 21% oxygen. That much nitrogen for an extended period of time would cause me to become lightheaded and ultimately to pass out. My job performance couldn't be trusted in case of emergency.

I knew I could do it. I knew I could overcome my physical shortcomings and do the job if given the chance. But the council didn't give me the chance to retake their tests or appeal their decision.

I didn't want to believe the results, so I did my own research. Had I spent my life in a mixed-gaseous environment, odds were high that I'd have adjusted to the atmosphere and this wouldn't have been an issue. But the amount of time I'd spent in the ice mines had made me more dependent on oxygen than I otherwise would have been. There were cases of this all over the universe. Coal miners on Earth who, instead of dying from pneumonoultramicroscopicsilicovolcanokoniosis, had learned to breathe the air deep inside the caves where they spent their days. Their illnesses came from deprivation of the air they'd developed a tolerance to, not from the air itself. It seemed that no matter what, I was destined to live out my life on Plunia.

Until I heard on the news that the uniform lieutenant had broken her leg while skiing on Mars and that the ship was looking for a last-minute substitute. I hacked into Federation Council's mainframe computer and copied my information on top of the name of the candidate they were about to confirm. I retrofitted a mining helmet with an air filter that cleaned seventy percent of the impurities out and blended what was left with a slow leak of oxygen that I fed from a tank I wore under my uniform. The Moon Unit boasted pure oxygen as one of the offerings at The

Space Bar, their restaurant and entertainment quarters, so once on the ship, it was just a matter of balancing my time in their air with time in my own. The way I saw it, getting onto the ship was ninety percent of the battle.

Until that darn navigation officer turned up in my closet. I'd checked, double-checked, and triple-checked every single thing that could have gone wrong. I'd never expected a murder.

Wait a minute. Why'd I think that? Why did my mind go to murder?

Of course. Of course! And if I could expose his killer, that had to prove to Neptune that I wasn't a threat. The captain would have to keep me on the ship. He'd probably give me a medal.

Emergency protocols on the ship stated that accidents, illnesses, and deaths were to be dealt with efficiently so as not to interrupt the vacation experience of the paying passengers. But if I was right—if the second navigation officer had been murdered—he deserved more than quick and quiet treatment. He was my coworker—or he would have been if he hadn't died. If it had been me, I'd want someone to care.

I had been the one to find the body, and that meant I knew things nobody else knew. I'd reported it as a Code Blue, but it wasn't just any Code Blue. It was a Code *Navy*

Blue. If the officer had been sick and died, he might have fallen to the ground. I might have found him behind a fixture or along the wall. I would not have found him *in* the closet *on top of* the folded uniforms. The placement of the body was intentional.

Nobody else knew exactly how he'd been hidden inside the closet before I opened the door. Except maybe Pika, who had vanished as quickly as she'd appeared the moment Yeoman D'Nar stepped into the uniform ward. Pika, who had seemed playful and bursting with childlike innocence. Pika, who had admitted that she wasn't supposed to be on the ship. Had that all been part of her Gremlon act? Was it possible that she'd committed murder on a whim and not realized the seriousness of her crime?

I looked away from the observation window, excited about my conclusions, until the sobering reality overwhelmed me.

A man had been killed. A stowaway had been present. Ship security was busy with an engineering problem and probably wouldn't even listen to me. But as long as the killer wandered the ship, none of us were safe.

Pika's desire to keep her presence on the ship secret would have given her motivation to silence him if he'd discovered her. I'd wanted to figure out one thing, and already I had two. What else did I know?

The BOP may have dictated that the second navigation officer's identity was defined by his position on the ship, but like I'd told Dr. Edison, I knew his position and rank because I recognized his uniform. He had two stripes on his cuff, which designated him as the second in charge, not the head of his division. If he'd found Pika in the uniform ward, he would have had a chance to turn her in before departure, but the bigger question was why was he there? If I was among the first regular crew members to board, how did he get there before me?

He had to have boarded the ship *before* I did. And the only people who were allowed on the ship before the general crew were security. Which meant the second navigation officer hadn't been there because he was excited about the departure like I was. He had something else in mind.

Something like sabotage. In engineering. The second navigation officer had been the threat Neptune was trying to discover.

6: UNEXPECTED INVITATION

I left the observation deck and took the elevator to the holding cell on the bottom floor. "Hey! Neptune!" I called out.

He seemed surprised to see me. "I told you to go to your quarters."

"I figured something out. Come on, listen to me. If I'm right, which I think I am, then your problems are over, which means *my* problems are over, because you won't need me to spy anymore so you can let me go back to my job in the uniform ward."

"You are still in my custody. You'll remain in my custody until the council decides what to do with you."

"But you made a mistake. I didn't do anything wrong! I mean, okay, there might be a problem with my application that we can straighten out at a less crucial time, but I'm not talking about me, I'm talking about

Dak—the second navigation officer. He's your problem, not me. He wasn't supposed to be in the uniform ward."

"Get into the cell."

I had willfully returned to the security level to help this security ape, and he was putting me back into holding?

Neptune pointed into the cell. I didn't have a lot of options. As soon as I crossed the threshold, he activated the beams. The heat that came off them made my lavender skin flush. I felt dizzy. I stepped farther into the cell to get away.

"You are impersonating a ship officer," Neptune said. "That's a second-degree offense and will be addressed by the council. It's up to the captain to decide whether we're going to drop you off on Colony 13 on our way to Ganymede or if it will be less disruptive to the passengers to keep you in custody and deal with you after we land."

"I didn't impersonate a ship officer. I never lied about who I was, and I never impersonated Daila Teron. Besides, the uniform lieutenant is *not* an officer. It's general crew. No privileges, no responsibilities aside from the tasks outlined in the BOP. Yeoman D'Nar is my supervisor, just like all the lieutenants on the ship. Did you notify her to tell her you arrested me? Because I'm pretty sure *that's* in the BOP somewhere. A senior officer is to be notified if one of her employees cannot perform their assignment. I can't perform my assignment from behind fire bars. If I don't show up, it's a reflection on her, and you can darn sure believe I'm going to let her know."

Neptune planted himself directly opposite me, crossing his arms and straining the fabric of his uniform. I briefly wondered if he had to have it specially made to fit his broad shoulders and massive biceps. I gave him a couple of seconds to speak. At that moment, I would have taken just about any response from him as a sign that he heard me. But he neither spoke nor moved. He stood there staring at me. Assessing me. Judging me.

"Ask Yeoman D'Nar if she hired me and she'll say yes. She addressed my orientation packet to Sylvia Stryker and signed my letter of acceptance right below the captain's signature." *So there*, I wanted to add.

Behind Neptune, a male voice came over the intercom. "Bridge to Security. Come in, Security."

Neptune went to the desk and hit a button. "Security, Neptune speaking."

"Neptune, it's Thaddeus. I need you to come to The Space Bar."

Thaddeus! The only Thaddeus I knew about was Captain Thaddeus Swift. Neptune was on a first name basis with the captain?

"I have a security situation," Neptune grunted in response.

The captain cleared his throat, and his voice became a little more formal. "Need I remind you that this is not a fighting vessel? It's a cruise ship. With passengers and entertainment. There's an open seat at First Dinner. Your presence is required. Your duties involve more than security situations. Non-negotiable. Over."

This time Neptune glared at me. He flipped the switch that activated the beams, and instantly they disappeared. "Come with me."

I hadn't expected Neptune to deactivate the security measures he'd put into place. According to the BOP, if I was indeed in custody, then I was supposed to be under surveillance at all times. For whatever reason, instead of calling in reinforcements to take over, it looked like he was letting me go. Aside from the sense that I'd scored a small victory, I was just plain curious.

I stepped out of the cell, and he pointed. "Walk."

A man of few words. I left the security area and approached the elevator. The doors swished open. I got in and crossed my arms. "I don't know where we're going."

"We're going to your quarters."

"Why?"

"Because I don't think you want the captain to see

you violating the uniform code."

"What does Captain Swift have to do with anything? It's probably dinner time. How's he going to see me? Won't he be dining with the paying passengers on board the ship?"

"We're going to dinner at The Space Bar. It's the first night of the journey, and Purser Frank requires a full banquet room. The second navigation officer has been unavoidably detained—" he paused, presumably to give me time to acknowledge that we weren't mentioning the details of what had happened to Lt. Dakkar out loud—"so there's an empty table."

"And you're taking his place," I guessed. He nodded. "What does that have to do with me?"

"You're in my custody." He held his square plastic passkey in front of the elevator scanner. "I trust when you prepared for the journey to the moon, you packed evening attire?"

"Just get me to my quarters. I'll figure something out." I crossed my arms, mimicking his body language, and pouted. We both stood there for a moment.

"Floor?"

"Oh, come on. You claim to know everything else about me. You probably already snuck into my quarters and went through my luggage."

"I'll let you lead the way."

"I can't activate the elevator because you took my passkey."

"What makes you think you need a passkey to get to your quarters?"

"Because you used your passkey to get us to the sublevels and according to the ship schematics"—oops, best not to elaborate on my knowledge of the ship's schematics—"just use your passkey to get us to level two."

Neptune seemed pleased. I was starting to wonder if the only time he smiled was when he caught people lying. Not a bad trait for a security officer. He pressed a series of buttons on the control panel. The doors swished shut, and the car moved sideways. I grabbed the rail to help keep my balance, too late, and bumped into Neptune. It was like bumping into a rock with a blanket wrapped around it.

"Sorry," I said quickly. I backed away two steps and held the railing tightly until the elevator car eased to a halt.

Neptune exited first. He turned to me. "You are to stay within five feet of me at all times. If you try to get away, I will advise the captain to drop you off at Colony 13 regardless of what it means to the paying passengers. Do you understand?"

"I didn't do anything wrong," I said for the thousandth time.

"Do. You. Understand?" he repeated.

"Yes."

Neptune stood back and indicated that I should lead the way. I assumed it was because he didn't trust me and thought I'd make a break for it if left behind. I reached my door and held my hand up to the panel outside of it. The doors swished open. I turned to him. "If I'm not supposed to be on this ship, how come the doors respond to my body chemistry?"

He didn't answer.

I went inside. On top of the table, next to a vase with a single Plunian flower, was a small robotic cat that I built when I was ten. It had turquoise ears and eyes, and when Neptune put his hand out toward it, it lifted its head and meowed. Neptune pulled his hand away in surprise. Too bad I hadn't programmed the cat to bite.

"Don't mind Cat. He only meows when he senses something near him that isn't me."

"How does it know I'm not you? Sound chip would work, but I haven't said anything."

"It reacts to voice *and* temperature." And fingerprint, but I wasn't going to tell Neptune that. No need to give away all my secrets. "He's a boy."

Neptune tipped his head and looked at Cat's butt. "How can you tell?"

"Because he can't have kittens."

He raised one eyebrow.

I opened the orange cabinet that held my extra uniforms and my off-duty clothes. I never expected to get invited to First Dinner on the ship. That was a privilege reserved for officers and passengers. The rest of the crew got our meals from the food machines in the employee lounge. There was nothing in the computer about how to dress when I wasn't working, and anything I might have found out through regular crew gossip would happen after tonight—which would be too late.

I turned and glared at Neptune. "You're not planning on standing there while I change, are you?"

"I'll be back in five minutes." He swiped his hand past the door panel, and the doors swished open. "Wear the blue one," he said over his shoulder, and left.

7: FIRST CHANCE TO SLEUTH

There was no way to check the locks on a spaceship. If Neptune was giving me time to change, then I was going to take it. I unhooked my collar at the back of my neck and shimmied out of my modified (torn) uniform. It fell to the floor in a metallic magenta pile. I kicked it off with the toe of my boot and then grabbed the aqua blue dress from the closet and pulled it over my head. I piled my dark hair on top of my head and secured it with a silver conical clip, letting the curly ends spill down over my crown. A quick glance in the mirror confirmed what I'd suspected, that the pale aqua made my lavender skin, in contrast, look radioactive. Here's hoping the passengers were open-minded.

The lack of quality oxygen all day had left me tired and short of breath. I reached into my luggage on top of the closet and pulled out a spare canister of O2. There wasn't a ton of time, so I inhaled and exhaled two deep breaths of it, hid it in the closet, and left my room. Neptune waited for me in the hallway.

In the short amount of time that it had taken me to transition from ship prisoner to crew member date at First Dinner, Neptune had undergone his own transformation. Gone were his coveralls, and in their place was a white dress uniform that consisted of a military-inspired jacket and trousers. The white fabric made his tawny skin stand out in contrast. The ship insignia was stitched onto the collar, but the garment was otherwise clear of bands to indicate rank or privilege. I assumed the lack of accoutrements had to do with his desire not to draw attention to himself.

My door swished shut behind me. The fabric of my dress caught in the door. Neptune held his hand up and the door open. I stepped away and smoothed the fabric down. The doors swished shut again. Neptune stepped closer to me and clamped a weighted metal bracelet around my left wrist. The same magnetic pull that I'd felt between my boots and the walls of the cell in the subbasement pulled my wrist toward the railing embedded to the ship's walls.

"What's this?"

"Cuff bracelet. You seemed under-accessorized." He

smiled that annoying joke-at-my-expense smile. "So you don't get any ideas."

I balled my fist and shook my arm a few times to see if I could make it fall off. (I could not.) "It doesn't go with this dress."

"Need I remind you that you're still in my custody?"

"No, you needn't," I said with a trace of annoyance.

Neptune stared at my outfit. "The dress looks...different than I expected."

"Is something wrong with it?"

"No. Let's go," he said. He didn't make eye contact.

I balled my fists up and held my arms in front of me. How was I supposed to know what was right for First Dinner? Neptune should have known, and he was the one who told me which dress to wear. And now that my arm was weighted down with a giant carbon security cuff, everybody would know I was in custody. If I looked bad, it was all his fault. The knowledge didn't particularly help me overcome my self-consciousness.

We arrived at the quarterdeck. The Space Bar was the ship's top-notch restaurant and entertainment hub. Sunken down three steps, the interior of the restaurant and lounge was carpeted in turquoise and fitted with aluminum tables and chairs. The ceiling was the darkest purple I'd ever seen. Filament lights hung from overhead, tiny luminous threads that exploded in light at the ends like clusters of stars in a manufactured nebula.

Ever since space travel became a thing, the world had changed. Well, not the world, but the whole universe. Somewhere in the late twenty-first century, earthlings had taken what they'd learned from decades of space exploration and colonized Mars. Shortly after, they'd branched out to Venus, Saturn, and beyond. There had been so many medical advances that the lifespan of earthlings had created an overpopulation that led many to relocate even outside of their solar system. It wasn't unusual to find interracial populations on any of the planets.

Inside The Space Bar, colorful couples and families sat in groups, some with officers of the ship and some alone. A kitchen staff member who looked like he was afraid of being seen maneuvered a handcart filled with a crate of aluminum tanks marked NO. I'd heard the Moon Unit leaked a mixture of nitrous oxide with oxygen during Happy Hour but until now hadn't believed it. The crew member pushed the cart behind a sparkling white floor-to-ceiling curtain, vanishing from my sight.

A hostess in a short white uniform and white gravity boots led Neptune and me to a table for two. The uniform guide indicated that employees in the passenger-facing aspects of the service industry were to wear white, and those who worked in the back wore black. The stark color coding might have seemed extreme, except that behind-the-scenes jobs lent themselves to stains. Even in space, practicality took precedence. My position as lieutenant of uniforms wasn't important enough for me to dine at The Space Bar. The only way I'd ever be seated in this room was as someone's date.

I waited until we'd both been served Saturnian wine before attempting small talk. "You're with ship security. How'd you get started in that field?"

Neptune looked up from his drink. "You don't have to make conversation."

"Just because you have no table manners doesn't mean I don't. My mother raised me right."

"And your father? What influence did Jack Stryker have on the way you turned out?"

"Fine. We can eat in silence."

The day after I'd hacked into the ship's computer, I worried about being caught. Had the Moon Unit been a government ship and not an entertainment vessel, the sentence would have been the placement of a tracking chip in my head, jail time on Colony 13, and a permanent mark on my record. Punishment for tampering with a cruise ship was a little murkier. The owners of the ship would have final say, and after the troubles with Moon Units 1 through 4, most likely they'd want to avoid a scandal. That's what I told myself when I couldn't sleep at night.

When the orientation packet arrived with a welcome letter signed by Captain Swift, it finally dawned on me that no one knew what I'd done. The computer said I was the replacement uniform lieutenant, and the computer was always right. From that point on, I filled out every document truthfully and submitted them by the deadline. My credentials arrived shortly after that, including my day one uniform, EZ guide of best practices for the ship, and a copy of the information I'd submitted. Nowhere on that application had I mentioned my dad's name. And Neptune had brought him up twice.

"If you have something to say to me about my father, then just come on out and say it."

"I'm not the one who expunged him from my personal history."

"There was no expungement. My dad wasn't relevant to my application. My mother raised me. She's my reference. She's the one who filled out and submitted my initial application."

"I know."

"See, I don't get that. How do you know? That

information was not made public. It's bound by Federation Council's Secrecy Act."

Unlike when we'd first arrived, Neptune appeared to enjoy the turn of the conversation. "I know more about you than you think, Stryker. Don't forget it."

I wadded my napkin in my lap and then clawed at the magnetic cuff around my left wrist. My efforts were useless.

The employee handbook had specified that senior officers were to remain in uniform at all times, and they'd been provided with standard issue garments to ensure compliance. To anybody who looked our way, I was Neptune's date.

He wished.

Around the rest of The Space Bar, sets of guests celebrated their first night on Moon Unit 5. It didn't take much effort on my part to mentally record the details. In spite of the fact that I was dining with a Neanderthal security officer who was blackmailing me, I was enjoying myself.

Mostly.

It took only a moment to realize my unexpected invitation to First Dinner came with the perfect opportunity to look for suspicious behavior. I sipped my wine and studied the other attendees.

Thanks to the Moon Unit policy of requiring officers to wear dress whites to dinner, I couldn't identify crew by the color of their uniforms. Not a problem, I thought to myself, but an opportunity. An opportunity to practice my powers of observation.

At the table to my left sat two green Martians. They wore dress whites, but the spectrometers dangling from the belts indicated they were part of the communication crew. Two tables past them Yeoman D'Nar sat with Purser Frank.

D'Nar looked at us and then looked away as if our table was still empty. The Yeoman's blond hair was in a pile on top of her head, and her dress and lipstick matched her pearlescent blue nail polish. Blue lipstick made me look cold. On her, it looked ethereal. I'd never been ethereal a day in my life.

Purser Frank, a friendly looking man with black hair and white glasses, was in charge of Moon Unit entertainment. He downed two glasses of wine before D'Nar had finished her first. Nerves, I assumed. Or the prospect of dining with Yeoman D'Nar required a little something extra to take the edge off. I snuck a glance at my dining companion. Guess I knew how Purser Frank felt.

The captain's table sat directly in front of the stage.

Captain Swift, a tall, thin man with fiery red hair and black glasses, looked at ease with the guests at his table. They so perfectly exemplified the target demographic of the newly revived Moon Units that they might as well have stepped off the pages of the promotional materials. Would the Moon Unit Corporation have hired stand-ins to play the part of cruise ship passengers to maintain their image? It was one way to ensure the standards on the ship. Captain Swift made a point of acknowledging Neptune's presence with a gesture to his own uniform and feigned applause to show he took note of Neptune's adherence to the dress code.

A woman in a long white dress approached our table. "Neptune." She squinted her eyes at me for a moment. "Who is your date?"

"Lt. Stryker," I said, smiling graciously. "Uniform ward."

"Ah, general crew." She turned to Neptune. "Still haven't learned, have you?" She leaned down closer to him. "You can act however you like in your quarters, but while you're in here, you are to keep your voice down and *pretend* to be civilized. The passengers don't know you're ship security and I don't want them to find out tonight. Guests of the captain have already commented on your intimidating presence. If you want to be invited to The

Space Bar again, I suggest you act like a guest, not like a bull in a china shop."

I closed my eyes and mentally flipped through the pictures I'd seen of Moon Unit's crew until I connected a name to the woman in front of us. "Uma?" I asked. *Quick, Sylvia, what else do you know about her?* "Uma Tolst. You're The Space Bar hostess. You trained under Captain Murray on the USS Charles."

"That's right," she said, surprised.

"You've done an impressive job with the dinner tonight." I raised my glass of Saturnian wine. "This is a particularly refreshing vintage. What will you be pairing it with?"

Uma stood up straighter. "Tonight is a special menu. Protein mix with a side of grains. Oxygen-infused dry ice cream for dessert."

"From Plunia?"

"Of course." She smiled and tapped the table by my plate. "Make sure Neptune uses his table manners. I wouldn't want to embarrass the captain at our First Dinner."

I smiled back. Uma left the table, and I looked at Neptune. "She seems to like you about as much as I do. What did you accuse her of?"

He glared at me and downed his glass of water. His

wine went untouched.

We spent the balance of the dinner in silence, not that I minded. I finished my glass of Saturnian wine and Neptune's too (he'd offered after a wee bit of prompting from me). His reprimand hung over my head, but the short conversation with the hostess had left my spirits high. I'd come across as refined compared to Neptune. Score one. And she served a mean bowl of ice cream. The oxygen charge in the dessert perked me up considerably.

By the time the plates were cleared, I was ready to sit back and enjoy the floor show. The general lights of the dining area dimmed, and a ring of pink bulbs glowed in a circle around the base of the stage. I was so engaged in what was happening that I didn't notice Captain Swift standing next to our table.

"Neptune," he said. "A word."

Neptune stood, and the two men conversed. The captain glanced at me and then returned to his table. Neptune pulled me out of my chair by my upper arm.

"Don't grab me," I said.

"Sabotage in engineering."

"That can't be. I tried to tell you, Lt. Dakkar was the saboteur and he's dead."

He glared at me. "We have to leave."

I moved his beefy paw from my arm to my hand.

"Better make it look good," I said. He pulled me past the guests just as the opening act, a shimmery gold woman draped in transfugitive silks, started to sing.

8: A NEW CRISIS

I had to practically jog to keep up with Neptune. "What's the problem?" I asked.

"Captain said maintenance confirmed a problem with the computer readings in engineering. Security protocol requires me to oversee the technicians while they work."

"We're going to miss the floor show? That's not fair. That woman was *gold*. Do you think she was painted? Or was she born that way? I've never seen a gold woman before." We were away from the crowd, so I pulled my hand out of his grip. "How about this. I'll go back to our table and watch the floor show. You do the security thing and come get me when you're done. If anybody asks about you, I'll say you're in the men's room."

"The BOP dictates that I can't leave a prisoner unsupervised."

The Saturnian wine had left me ever so slightly

buzzed. I jabbed my finger into Neptune's chest and pouted. "You're not going to keep calling me a prisoner, are you?"

The ship tilted, and we both stumbled. I felt a vibration under the soles of my boots. When I looked up, I saw a new expression on Neptune's face. I didn't know what it meant, but I knew it wasn't a joke.

"Come on." He turned and ran down the hallway to the elevator.

"We're not done talking about this," I said under my breath.

As we rounded the corner, it wasn't hard to see that things were more critical than I'd thought. Emergency bulbs mounted on the walls cast the room in a bath of red. With a sweeping glance, I counted two men passed out on the ground and a panel of blinking buttons on the computer that the men should have been monitoring. The red lights canceled out everything but the glow of the buttons, and almost immediately I recognized that the warning lights indicated a problem with the hull. I stepped over one of the bodies and prepared to override the system with a manual entry when Neptune pulled me away from the computer.

"Don't touch it."

"But there's a problem with the hull. You said it

yourself, earlier, when you were in the uniform ward. I heard you. You thought you fixed it, but you didn't. There must be a gas leak making these men unconscious."

He looked from me to the computer panel. I knew I was right. Apparently, Neptune recognized that I was right too. He shifted me out of the way and overrode the system. A loud alarm rang out, a series of *Woop! Woop! Woop!* sounds that made it difficult to hear anything else. One of the men on the ground stirred and grabbed my ankle. Instinctively I kicked his hand away. He locked eyes with me and grabbed at his throat like he was choking.

He was suffocating. I grabbed Neptune's arm and pointed at the man. Neptune abandoned the computer and broke into a locked case of oxygen canisters. He threw one to the man on the ground, who pulled the pin and inhaled the pure air.

The noise level was deafening. Piercing sirens on repeat bounced off the walls, reverberating back at me and echoing inside my head. Neptune dropped to the ground and forced the other men to inhale from the oxygen canisters. I knew I wasn't supposed to do anything. I knew he wanted me to stand to the side of the room and wait until he had things under control. I knew right now I was yet another problem Neptune thought he had to handle and the more I stayed out of the way, the better off he'd be. At least, I suspected it. But what Neptune didn't know because he wouldn't listen to me was that I could be of help. There wasn't time to try to explain it. Not when I could demonstrate my skills and deal with the consequences after the crisis was over.

I hiked my aqua dinner dress up to mid-thigh and stepped over one of the bodies on the floor to get to the computer. It took a moment to remember the code sequence. I pressed two white buttons to the left and the red one to my right. The alarm shifted from *Woop! Woop!* to a more subdued *Beep! Beep!* and the red lights turned off. A moment later, they flashed on the far side of the room. I went to the wall and ran my fingers over it. In a matter of seconds, I located a tiny plastic hose jutting out from between two panels. I held my fingers in front of the opening and felt a stream of gas escaping from it.

There was no issue with computer readings. Someone had purposely rigged a gas leak in the engineering room.

I tried to get Neptune's attention. He squatted next to the first officer and held the oxygen container to his mouth. The oxygen would revive the men temporarily, but we needed to move them, or they'd pass out as soon as Neptune removed the tank.

I ran forward and grabbed Neptune's arm. He looked

angry. I pointed to the wall where the plastic tube was hidden He pushed me back. I stumbled into the computer. I grabbed Neptune's wrist with both hands and leaned back with my full weight. He barely budged.

I let go with one hand and pointed again, and then hollered, "Gas leak! Get them out of here!" but the siren was too loud, and even I couldn't hear myself. I dropped Neptune's arm and ran to the wall. The only way to keep more gas from leaking into the room was to divert it. I put the plastic tube to my mouth and inhaled it into my lungs.

Neptune's eyes widened when he realized what I'd been trying to tell him. He lifted the officer next to him and carried him the way we'd come. Seconds later he returned and repeated the routine for the next officer. My eyes blurred with tears from inhaling the noxious gas. I had to make it a few seconds more, a few seconds until I could erase the toxins with a hit from the oxygen canister on the ground.

I put my thumb over the end of the hose to keep it from spewing out more gas and tried to hold my breath, but it was too late. The lack of pure oxygen in the ship, my being without my filtration helmet, and whatever I'd inhaled from the hose to keep the leak from further contaminating the air in the engineering room clouded my mind. I let go of the hose to put my hands over my ears and my legs buckled underneath me. I collapsed onto the floor and the world went black.

9: TOYING WITH THE TRUTH

I woke up in the holding cell. I was on the narrow cot clutching a canister of pure O2. Pika the Stowaway was curled up in the shadows in the corner of the cell. She still wore the gray flex crew uniform I'd given her, but the grime was gone from her face.

"How did I get here?" I asked warily. This was the second time the pink Gremlon had shown up in a place she shouldn't have been and that alone was suspicious. I wasn't ready to trust her yet.

"You're awake! You're awake! You're awake!" Pika said. She jumped up and bounced back and forth from one foot to the other. "Shhhhhhh," she said. "We have to be quiet."

I shifted my weight and sat up. Someone removed my boots, and they sat along the wall at the back of the cell. My feet were cold against the painted black floor. "What happened?"

Pika dropped down to a squat and looked at me. "I went looking for you. You were in the engineering room. The giant picked you up and carried you here."

"Did he see you?"

"No. I'm good at hiding." She smiled sheepishly. "I followed him so I could see where he took you before."

I wasn't ready to trust her, but, at the moment, she knew more than I did about my circumstances. I leaned forward and looked out of the cell. The beams hadn't been activated, and Neptune wasn't at his security station. "Where did the giant go?"

Pika shrugged. "I don't know. He carried you in here and put you on the bed and then left. Uh-oh!" Pika dropped down to the floor and rolled under the bed. Seconds later, Doc Edison came around the corner with Yeoman D'Nar and Neptune.

"Lt. Stryker," Doc said. "I've been expecting you in the medical ward. When you didn't show, I went to your supervisor."

Yeoman D'Nar stood next to him, unsmiling. I wasn't particularly in a smiley mood either. The ship had departed less than twenty-four hours ago, and already I'd determined my three least favorite people on the ship. Worse, they were all in front of me. I looked back and forth between the doc and my boss, and then at Neptune, who stood slightly behind them. His surprise-you're-going-to-lockup visit had been the main reason I'd never made it to the medical ward, but my boss and the doc didn't seem to know about that. Why not?

Neptune moved forward and held out my helmet. "I found this in the uniform ward. I trust it's yours."

"Thank you." I took the clear plastic bubble and wrapped my arms around it. Until I had a chance to check that it wasn't cracked and reattach the oxygen hose, it wasn't going to do me any good. And as long as I had an audience of people who could potentially have me booted from the ship, I was going to pretend I wore the helmet for cosmetic reasons. Hey, it could happen. I'd seen stranger accessories in a catalog of Venusian fashions.

I felt weird sitting on my cot while the three senior officers stood in front of me, but I also knew Pika was underneath my cot, and there was a better chance of her staying hidden if I didn't stand up. Pika was the only one of the four of them who hadn't yelled at me or accused me of something. That put her on my side.

I got the feeling Doc Edison and Yeoman D'Nar expected me to say or do something, but since I wasn't sure of what (the BOP didn't have a protocol for post-passing out after discovering sabotage aboard the ship), I didn't say or do anything. Seconds passed. My hands grew sweaty on the plastic bubble of my helmet and slipped down the convex surface. I wiped my lavender palm on the side of my aqua dress and then wrapped my arms around the helmet again.

Yeoman D'Nar spoke first. "Security section has advised me of your assistance in the engineering room. Dr. Edison will check your vital signs."

"I'm all right," I said. "Nothing a good night's sleep in my quarters won't fix. I'll be good as new tomorrow."

"You won't be spending the night in your quarters," Neptune said. Three lines appeared between his eyebrows, and he tipped his chin down. His forehead took over the top half of his face.

"Until security section can debrief you on what happened in the engineering room, you'll remain in Neptune's custody," D'Nar added.

"What? No! I want to go to my room."

Neptune crossed his arms and stood with his feet shoulder-width apart. He looked at me and then at Doc. "Lt. Stryker seems to be doing better. I need to take her report while things are fresh in her mind. Can this physical wait until tomorrow?"

Doc glared at him. "It's not a good idea to put off the health of the crew while we're in flight," he muttered. He reached into his bag and pulled out a second canister marked O2. "After the ape is done with you, breathe this. It's pure oxygen and will equalize your lungs and drive out whatever you inhaled down there in the engineering room. Come see me tomorrow for a complete workup." He smiled warmly. "Thank you, Lt. Stryker. What you did may have saved the lives of two men on the crew."

I set my helmet on the ground and took the canister. Doc closed his bag and turned to leave. "Yeoman, are you coming?"

"Not yet," she said. "Who's going to manage the uniform ward? I can't. I have other responsibilities on this ship."

Neptune spoke. "Uniform Ward will remain closed until I say so."

"But the crew—" she started.

"Fine. I'll take over the uniform ward. It's my call."

Yeoman D'Nar didn't look happy with Neptune's answer, but she also didn't look like she thought she'd win in a battle against him.

Doc Edison and Yeoman D'Nar left. I sat on the cot and waited—for what, I didn't know. The doors at the end of the hall swished open and shut. Neptune remained in front of me with his arms crossed over his chest.

"Get out," he said.

"Get out from where? You just told them I was spending the night here!"

"Not you. The Gremlon. Get out from under the cot."

My helmet bumped forward on the floor and Pika rolled out. She stood up, a little disheveled, but still relatively pleasant. "I'm sorry, Mr. Giant."

"Get lost," Neptune said, jerking his thumb over his shoulder toward the hallway. "I don't want to see you in here again."

Pika took off without being asked twice. As soon as she was around the corner, Neptune hit the button on the wall, and the blue beams of light appeared. I stepped backward to avoid the heat.

"Why didn't you lock her up?" I asked.

"She's no threat."

"She's a stowaway."

Neptune glared at me. "I'll be back," he said. He turned around and left the direction Pika had gone.

As soon as I was alone, I pulled the pin on the O2 canister and inhaled. Pure oxygen flooded my lungs. It felt like an itch I couldn't scratch from somewhere deep within me had been doused in a calming agent. I closed my eyes and held the air in my lungs for a few seconds before exhaling. The irritation subsided, and I relaxed. I didn't want to overdo it. The sooner I became acclimated to the air on the ship, the easier it would be for me to do my job without raising questions. *More* questions. Neptune already knew too much about me, but to the rest of the ship, I was just another employee. I wanted it to stay like that.

See, that didn't make sense. If Neptune knew I'd hacked my way into the position on the ship, why hadn't he told Yeoman D'Nar or Doc Edison? The physical would have outed me even before breathing the toxic air in the engineering room. Neptune must have had some other reason to keep my secret for now. He threatened me with prison time on Colony 13, but hadn't mentioned that to my boss or the doc. Why not? It was starting to feel like Neptune was keeping an eye on me for reasons other than protocol.

As the oxygen erased the effects of the gas, my thoughts became clearer. I'd been on the ship for less than a day, and already there were questions I hadn't expected to have to answer. It was the job of the security officer to make sure the ship was safe, and twice now, security had failed.

As the convulsions in my lungs subsided, I stood up and wandered back and forth across the ten-foot by ten-foot cell. Without the minor annoyance of the magnetic floor and the gravity boots, I felt light, which gave weight to my thoughts in contrast. *Go back, Sylvia. Go back to your first minutes on the ship.* What had I figured out? The second navigation officer had no reason to be on the ship when he was, and earlier I'd concluded that he was there to sabotage it. Pika had been in the very same quarters. Lt. Dakkar could have been the one to set up the gas leak in the engineering quarters, and Pika could have been there to help him. But Pika was given the run of the ship while Neptune treated me like a criminal. That made no sense. Unless Neptune knew more about the murder of the second navigation officer than he claimed.

Neptune had shown up in the uniform ward despite D'Nar dismissing my report to the bridge. Almost like he'd already known what he'd find when he arrived.

There was only one department on this entire ship that could terminate a crew member if assessed to be a threat and not be challenged on their action. Security. And who was security? Neptune.

Neptune didn't care about the murder in the uniform ward. Maybe I'd been wrong. Maybe *he* was the one with something to hide.

10: WHO TO TRUST?

I crept close to the beams of blue-hot light and looked back and forth for signs of security. For all Neptune's talk about keeping me under surveillance, he'd activated the beams, but then he left. If he considered me a real threat, he wouldn't have just walked away. That meant he felt comfortable. Secure that I didn't suspect him of anything.

I returned to the cot and inhaled more oxygen. Was I thinking clearly yet? I didn't know. But I couldn't deny the fact that Neptune's behavior was suspicious.

I'd trained myself to break problems down into what I knew so I could isolate the unknown variables and attack them. I had nothing to take notes on, so I cleared my mind and focused.

What I knew: Neptune had arrived at the uniform ward shortly after I'd called the bridge about the Code Blue. Yeoman D'Nar had dismissed my report. I'd assumed she'd called him anyway, but this was not about what I'd assumed. It was about what I knew. Neptune arrived quickly. He knew the victim. He later returned and removed me and sealed off the uniform ward.

Possible explanations: He discovered the second navigation officer's plan to sabotage the ship and took out the threat to the passengers. He was already close to my sector when I radioed the bridge, so he intervened. He sealed off the uniform ward after removing me so he could destroy any evidence of his actions.

It was possible. More than possible. My years at the space academy had taught me that professional dedication to the job trumped everything. Neptune was the head of security for the revived Moon Unit Cruise Ships. He would not have gotten that job by playing it safe. What I needed was access to a computer where I could pull his files and see exactly how far he'd gone in the name of professional job fulfillment in the past. If I could find evidence that murder was an acceptable part of the job to him, then I'd know for sure.

I rose and approached the hot light beams again. My Plunian core temperature allowed me to get closer to the flames than other people might have gotten, and when I angled myself from the far corner of the cell, I could make out an empty desk at the end of the hallway. The surface was clean and smooth except for a small plastic dome on the right corner that covered a red button, just like I'd had in the uniform ward. Next to the plastic dome was a series of square buttons that lit up in intervals. Red, green, and yellow. From the schematics I'd downloaded from the space library before we left, I knew they were call buttons to different parts of the ship. If I could get closer, I could map the panel in my mind and figure out how it worked. For two little letters, "if" was a really big word.

In the history books that I'd studied in grade school before being accepted to the space academy, I'd learned about what life was like for people who grew up on Earth. There were countries with governments and laws, punishments for behavior that wasn't considered appropriate. People weren't allowed to kill other people under most circumstances. The laws didn't stop the murders from happening, though, which was why Federation Council had come up with a different solution to the problem.

When someone was suspected of a crime, they were tried in front of the council. Twenty-three members heard every case, deliberated, and decided on an appropriate course of action. Smaller colonies in the galaxy became designated living spaces for those who the council deemed unsuitable for life among the planets.

I didn't know this last part from a class in middle school. I knew it because of my dad. He'd been charged with colluding with space pirates to raise demand for the dry ice from our mines. He pled guilty. We'd gone from being saviors to opportunists.

He'd been sent to Colony 13 to live with others who'd turned against their own people. The federation council had determined that anyone who would put his needs ahead of what was best for his planet didn't deserve the freedom he'd inherited. I'd memorized the names of each of the council members who had voted to send my dad away for his crime. Twenty-two out of twenty-three had found him guilty.

Only one had recused himself from the vote. Vaan Marshall. He was the youngest member of Federation Council and that had been his first case.

He'd also been my first real boyfriend.

After the ruling, we broke up. Whether Vaan's recusal from the vote was one of inexperience or loyalty to me, I'd never know. But dating a member of the council that had banished my dad to Colony 13, even if my dad *had* violated the governing code of Federation Council, wasn't something I could do. It was hard enough to live with the knowledge that my dad was a criminal. I didn't need a reminder of the group that sent him away.

But right now, it would have come in handy to know someone in Federation Council. Well, it would have come in handy if I wasn't currently behind bars myself.

The elevators in the hallway swished open and shut. I braced myself for Neptune's presence. Now that I had concerns along scarier lines than he's-a-pain-in-my-butt type, I wasn't looking forward to spending more time with him. When Doc Edison rounded the corner instead of Neptune, I relaxed.

Doc pushed the button on the wall outside the cell and the beams of light retracted into the ceiling and floor. "Between you and me, I don't know why that big ape thinks you need to be secured in here. You saved two men from suffocation. That makes you a hero in my book and don't think I haven't already made a report to Captain Swift. Have a seat. Let's get you cleared for active duty so you can sleep in your own bed tonight."

He pulled a small scanner out of his bag and held it above my head, parallel to the floor, and then slowly brought it down past my eyes, nose, mouth. He asked me to breathe into a tube, and then he pulled out an ominous-looking device that looked suspiciously like a needle. Instinctively, I leaned away.

"What's that?"

"I need a sample of your blood."

"Why? I didn't cut myself. I inhaled a toxic gas. If there are any long-term effects from the gas, they're going to restrict my respiratory system, not my circulation."

"I'm aware of that, and the preliminary tests I've already run indicate your respiratory problems are self-healing. What I'm more concerned about is the fact that you are part Plunian and I don't have an active panel on you in the medical lab."

"But you must. I had to have a physical to be approved to work aboard Moon Unit 5," I said carefully.

"You have extensive knowledge of the regulations and requirements of working aboard the ship, Lt. Stryker. And from what I saw earlier this evening when you helped the security ape in the engineering room, I'd say you're an asset to the crew. But unless you allow me to draw your blood, run up a panel, and override the falsified documents that are currently in the mainframe, Neptune is going to keep you locked up in this cell. And, since I'm pretty sure you share my doubts about his loyalties, I don't think either one of us wants that to happen."

11: PHYSICAL

Doc Edison reached for the wrist that still wore the thick magnetic cuff. He flipped my hand so it was palm-side up. His eyes took in the security bracelet and then returned to my face. I slowly extended my arm to make it easier for him to draw the blood he needed.

When he finished, he removed the vial from the needle and sealed it with a plastic cap, covered the cap with reflective security tape, and dropped the whole thing into a small bag that he also sealed. He nestled the vial in a black case filled with gray foam and sealed that too. He picked up his scanner and wanded it over the spot on my arm where the needle had been. The pinprick healed in seconds.

"I'd say I have everything I need. I'll notify Yeoman D'Nar that you'll be in your quarters for the duration of the night." He closed his medical bag and stood up. "Good evening, Lt. Stryker."

I kept my eyes on the magnetic floor by his feet. "Thank you, Doc."

He put his finger under my chin and raised my face. "You did a brave thing tonight. Neptune is an idiot. We need *more* crew members like you, not less." He smiled. "Now the important question: sugar pop or sugar shot?"

"Pop," I said.

He handed me a blue sugar pop. "Hang tight. You'll be back in your quarters soon." He turned around and left.

The realization that he knew my secret and wasn't going to turn me in overwhelmed me. I took the sugar pop to the small sink and ran water over the outside of it to dissolve the sanitary casing, and then stuck it into my mouth. The pure sugar would help return my body to its normal equilibrium after having given blood. Other members of the crew might have chosen the shot because it was immediate. Plus, sugar pops were associated with kids. After everything that had happened today, I didn't much mind taking a moment to return to the days when it felt like someone else was taking care of me.

A few minutes after the doc left, the doors to the elevator swished open, and the entertainment director who had been dining with Yeoman D'Nar walked in. He wore the same dress whites he'd had on at First Dinner. I would have expected him to change as soon as he could to avoid getting it soiled.

The entertainment director pushed his white glasses up the bridge of his nose with his pointer finger and then stepped into the cell and held out his hand. "We haven't been formally introduced. I'm Purser Frank."

"Sylvia Stryker."

"I know. I heard about what happened in engineering tonight. Doc asked me to escort you to your quarters."

"I'm sorry if I—we—disrupted the dinner service. From what I saw before we left, it was going to be an exceptional opening night."

"Opening night is a bit of a testing ground. Meet the passengers, mingle, find out what it is they want from their trip aboard Moon Unit 5. A surprising number of them asked when the nitrous oxide would be released." He chuckled. "Someday I'll find out how those rumors get started."

"So there's no laughing gas in The Space Bar? I thought I saw tanks of it being wheeled in."

"You must have been mistaken. Oxygen—that's what keeps people alert and vibrant. One hundred percent pure oxygen is piped in from the minute we open at Zulu Sixteen until we close at Zulu Two."

Zulu Sixteen referred to the sixteenth hour after midnight on the ship. Zulu time had been adopted on most spaceships because the personnel came from various planets, and interplanetary travel had become the norm. The hour the ship was sealed became Zulu Zero, and we all operated on Zulu time until we were docked at the space station regardless of where we'd come from. It was the best way to keep us all in sync.

"I didn't realize The Space Bar was open that late."

"We adjust the hours as needed by the guests. And don't spend another minute worrying about the distraction. Captain Swift told me he instructed Neptune to get to engineering. I wouldn't have expected Neptune to care much either way about leaving his date alone at the table. He gets points for taking you with him."

I started to protest and explain that Neptune and I hadn't been on a date until it occurred to me that Neptune had ample opportunities to clear that up himself. According to Neptune, I had to go with him because I was in his custody. If he was keeping that a secret from the other members of the ship, then he must have a reason. And the only reason I could come up with was that he didn't have grounds to hold me in the cell. Explaining my temporary incarceration would have put him in a negative light. Maybe I could use this to my advantage.

I stood up and followed the purser out of the sublevel, onto the elevator, and up to my floor. We turned left and walked side by side to my quarters. It was late, and the halls were empty. We had six more days of travel before reaching Ganymede. The captain and his first officers would be off tonight which meant the second in command of each station would be on the bridge.

"Purser Frank, who's responsible for taking over duties of the second navigational officer?"

"What do you mean?"

"The second nav officer was dead in the uniform ward earlier today. I was the one who found him, and I reported it to the bridge. I just realized that the first officers were all required to be at First Dinner, which means the second in command would be on the bridge, wouldn't they? But with no second navigation officer, who would be responsible for keeping us on course?"

"Funny you should ask. Yeoman D'Nar stepped into that role. Her degree in general space sciences made her the most qualified person on the ship."

"But she was with you at First Dinner."

"Only to make an appearance. She left shortly after you and Neptune did."

"Is that why she didn't come get me herself? The uniform ward is under her umbrella of responsibility, and

I would have expected her to know where I was and why I was there. With her additional responsibilities, will she still be my boss?"

"Temporarily. We have a stop scheduled at the next space station."

I stopped outside of my door. "I thought Moon Unit 5 went directly to Ganymede? Won't the passengers be alarmed if we start making unscheduled stops?"

The purser held his finger up to his mouth and then pointed to my door. I waved my hand over the sensor and the doors swished open. We went inside. The doors swished shut.

"This isn't public knowledge, but they told me you know what's been going on."

"A little. Why?"

"Just this. The captain is concerned. He arranged a stop off on Colony 5. He's telling passengers it's a chance to shop for space souvenirs, but Federation Council is sending a representative to join us for the duration of the trip. Once Neptune makes an arrest, he'll place them in the custody of Federation Council representative, who will take charge of them until we land at our final destination. The ship will be safe and the crew can focus on their jobs. And if one of our own is responsible for the crimes, then having a neutral party on board will eliminate any possible loyalties that have already formed."

"Sounds like the captain thought of everything."

"This was Neptune's plan. He said it all fell into place after he spoke to Federation Council about what happened tonight."

"He didn't," I said.

"He did. Captain Swift wants to keep details quiet from the passengers, but he ordered Neptune to call the federation and see about getting you a commendation for your role in the crisis. From what I understand, they were very interested in your act of bravery."

Of course, they were. Because as far as Federation Council knew, I had no place being on the ship. Neptune, the jerk, had figured out a way to have me removed from Moon Unit 5 without even having to do the dirty work himself. Worse, I was going to be arrested by the same people who had convicted and banished my dad.

"Did they tell you who they were going to send?" I asked. Might as well start prepping now for the inevitable comments about my dad and resulting judgment and humiliation. At least if I could dig up some background on whoever was joining us, I'd be able to prepare a defense.

"Yes. The Council is sending their youngest member, Vaan Marshall."

I didn't know whether to laugh or cry. If that was

true, Neptune had made a bad decision. Vaan was the one person who would know I'd gotten the post on board the ship through possibly illegal methods. Before he'd gone straight and been accepted onto Federation Council, he was a better hacker than I was. In hacking, just like in love, Vaan Marshall taught me everything I knew.

12: NEW PROBLEMS

At the mention of Vaan's name, Cat's eyes glowed and he eeked out an automated meow. Purser Frank jumped. He looked at the robotic cat on the table. Cat jiggled from foot to foot. I was pretty sure a coil had broken inside of Cat, which kept him from actually moving forward or back. I picked him up and covered his solar panel. His eyes went dark, and the vibration stopped.

I hadn't talked to Vaan since the breakup. It was inevitable that we'd see each other again because that's how these things went. It was just my luck that our reunion would take place while I was little more than a blackmailed stowaway on a spaceship with a murderer. It didn't get much worse than that.

I thanked Purser Frank for escorting me to my quarters and then said goodnight. It had been a long day, and I wanted to change out of my now mangled blue evening dress. I doubted there would be any more opportunities for me to dress for dinner, so it didn't much matter that this particular outfit was beyond repair.

After changing into my sleeping uniform, a loose-fitting jumpsuit with the same Moon Unit insignia that had been on my working uniform, I pulled covers back from the bed and slipped between them. The bedding was made of a new synthetic fabric that adjusted to individual body temperatures within five seconds. The designers of the Moon Unit series of ships had considered every way possible to keep the crew's supplies lightweight so paying passengers could bring whatever they felt they'd need to make their stay comfortable. Because of that, my room was compact. In addition to the bed, there was the white table where Cat sat, a matching chair, and the closet unit. My orientation packet had arrived with an empty standard-issue crew suitcase and instructions only to bring what would fit inside. Like everything else that related to the Moon Unit, the suitcase had the ship's insignia emblazoned on the outside. The architects of the ship might have had trouble with the first four in their fleet, but the one thing they'd worked out was branding.

The thin layer of heat-sensitive fabric on top of me adjusted to my Plunian core temperature and I closed my eyes. So much had happened in one day and I had six more to go. The last thing I remember thinking was what could possibly happen tomorrow?

***

I woke to Cat's meow on repeat. When I built him, I used parts from a broken alarm clock. The ship had been programmed to go on full light at Zulu Five, and since Cat's operations were fueled by a solar panel, his wake-up meow had been triggered. I threw my pillow across the room at him, and he went silent. Thank the galaxy for small favors and good aim.

The crew's quarters had standard-issue isolation chambers where purified atoms bombarded us and prepared us for our full day of work. It was the first day that my coworkers and I would jockey for position. I had Cat to thank for the fact that I was among the first there.

I stripped, activated the isolation chamber, and rotated for the required thirty seconds, then dressed in my day two uniform and headed to the employee lounge. A wall of food service machines offered wake-up beverages and protein packs. I inserted my ID card in front of the first machine and pressed the button. Nothing happened. I tried two more times with no success. It could have been a computer malfunction. Three little green Martians, members of the communication crew, came in, and I stepped aside. They each activated the very machine I couldn't get to work.

It wasn't a computer malfunction.

One of the communication crew members, a friendly looking Martian with sandy blond hair and freckles, stood to the side and waved me forward. "You were here first," he said. "Besides, I'm still deciding between blue protein and green protein. Depending on what you want, you might make my choice a little easier."

I stepped forward and inserted my card into the machine again. Again, nothing happened. The Martian leaned closer. "Did you break it?" he said.

"No! No. I mean, I don't think so. My card's been giving me trouble."

"Let me see it," he said.

Reluctantly, I held out my card. The little green man lifted a small device from the side of his belt and fed my card into it. "What are you doing?" I asked.

"Relax. I'm checking to make sure it's not demagnetized."

He held the device up and watched the screen. A series of colorful lights flashed in a somewhat random pattern, and then the machine beeped repeatedly. Two additional Martians joined him.

"Beryn, what's going on?" one asked.

"I don't know. This Plunian couldn't get her card to work in the machine, so I scanned it."

Beryn kept his eyes on the screen while the other Martians stared at me. I felt like a space amoeba in a Petri dish. I wanted my card, but it was in Beryn's machine and short of grabbing it from him and running, I didn't know how to get it back.

Beryn looked up. "Your card has a security flag on it. You're being tracked." The little green men stepped away from me, but Beryn didn't eject my card. "I heard some of the officers talking about a crime committed on the ship yesterday. They think there's an imposter on board."

This time I stepped back, away from the group. Our initial encounter had been conversational, but I knew from the BOP that if these men had reason to believe I—or anybody—was acting without Moon Unit's mission top of mind, they were in their rights to subdue me. And even though their small Martian stature made them appear less than threatening, there was the unfortunate ten-to-one ratio that wasn't in my favor.

I looked around the room. Even though I'd been on the early side, the cafeteria was now near capacity, filled with over twenty crew members. My brain imprinted with the colors of their uniforms and in a second cataloged them: medical, communications, supply, and flex. Not a single face was familiar. Or friendly. I backed away from them, first one step, and then two.

Beryn wasn't willing to let me leave that easily. He grabbed my wrist. My nerves had turned my temperature hot and seconds after he touched my skin, he pulled his hand away. "What are you, some kind of freak?" he asked. He looked around the room. "She burned me. Who let a stupid Plunian onto the ship anyway?"

Two other Martians grabbed my arms and held me into place. I twisted to get loose but couldn't. Beryn pulled a spectrometer off his belt and held it up. "There's one way to find out if you're the impostor. Get a sample of your blood and analyze the spectrum."

I wriggled to free myself, but more small green hands held me from behind. The tip of Beryn's spectrometer was a centimeter from my arm. He could pierce my skin with the flick of his thumb and gain a sample if he wanted. There was no telling what would happen to me if he did.

13: CLOSE CALL

"Get away from her," said a familiar voice from the doorway. It would have scared the crap out of me if I wasn't pretty scared already.

Neptune.

The men who held me in place dropped my arms. I was still thrashing about, and the sudden freedom from their grip sent me off-kilter and into Beryn. His spectrometer sent an electrical pulse through my arm. I jerked with a reactive spasm and fell.

"She doesn't belong here," Beryn said after glancing at the reading.

Neptune turned to Beryn and put his giant hand on the communication's officer's throat. He pushed him back through the crowd until Beryn was up against the food machines. "She's my responsibility," Neptune said. He yanked the spectrometer out of Beryn's hands. Neptune grabbed my arm and pulled me off the floor, stumbling out of the cafeteria behind him. Neither one of us spoke until he had me back in my quarters.

"What was that about?" he asked. He looked angry.

"You. This." I thrust my arm out in front of me to remind him of the bracelet. "Is this thing ever coming off?"

He raised his arm like he was checking the time on his watch, spun the dial counterclockwise and pressed a small, flat button. The bracelet clicked open and fell onto the floor, narrowly missing my toe. I pulled my foot back and then bent down and grabbed the bracelet and shoved it into Neptune's open hand. "Did you revoke my clearance?"

"Clearance for what?"

"For everything! I wanted to get breakfast before starting my shift, and my card didn't work. How come? I called the bridge when I found a body in my ward. And I helped save the life of two members of the engineering crew. Everything I've done since I arrived has been for the good of the ship, and you know it." I poked my index finger into his massive chest to punctuate the *you-know-it*. I wanted to storm away from him, but we were in my quarters, and the only place to go was the other side of the room. I crossed the small area and picked the pillow up from the floor. Cat rolled into a half circle and meowed at Neptune.

His expression changed from anger to surprise. Both eyebrows all but jumped from down low over his eyes to up high, causing a series of creases to appear on his forehead. Moments later, his normally stern expression dropped back into place.

"I don't know how you know the BOP. I don't know how you knew where the holding cell was. I don't know how you got credentials to be on this ship in the first place. What I *do* know is that your skill set makes you valuable to me."

"We covered that when you blackmailed me. Did anybody ever tell you you're a jerk?"

"I'm the jerk who just saved you from a Martian lynching in the cafeteria." He tapped the spectrometer he'd taken from Beryn. "This equipment is about to malfunction. If it had operated as expected, your spectrometer reading would have gotten you banished to the same prison where your dad is incarcerated. Or is that what you want?"

"No," I said somewhat stubbornly.

"Then take this." He reached into his back pocket and

pulled out a flat disc. Even from a few feet away, I could tell it was my ID card.

"You stole my ID card? The one I had was fake?" I glared at him. "Is that why mine didn't work in the machines?"

"It wasn't a fake. I had it deactivated. I thought I'd get to you before you used your old card. I'm giving you a new set of credentials that put you under the security section. I pulled your background, and that's where you belong."

"Why? Why protect me? Why make it look like I belong twenty-four hours after you arrested me?"

"We've had too much trouble since departing. Federation Council is sending a representative. I need to know if it's coincidence that they sent us the one person who recused himself from the vote to banish your father."

Neptune all but admitted he knew the history between Vaan and me. Great. Now there would be no pretending we were strangers.

"Next time you want to know something about me, try asking. There's no need to use the ship's computer for background checks on half-breed daughters of criminals."

He slapped the new ID card on the table. "I expect to see you in security section by Zulu Seven. Make sure you're wearing the right uniform." He turned around and left.

I waited until the doors swished shut behind Neptune to look at my new identification card. It had the same picture as my old one. To the right of my picture was my name, and under that were the words "Security Section." I flipped the card over. On the back was the magnetic strip that activated the vending machines, along with a small gold chip that gave me additional classifications. It was heavier than my old ID. According to what I'd learned while studying about the Moon Unit, only crew members with senior clearance had cards with chips. General ID cards were disposable and deactivated between flights.

Well, well. Neptune was still a jerk, but he was a jerk who had given me senior level clearance.

I put my pillow on the bed and put Cat on the pillow. Time to go to the uniform ward and change my outfit— and sneak one of the protein bars I'd hidden in the cabinet next to the BOP.

The morning encounters in the cafeteria had left me feeling self-conscious. It was one thing to have trouble with my ID card. It was quite another to be called names and surrounded by fellow crew members who appeared ready to turn me in. The trip to the moon was going to be a lonely one if I didn't make some friends. At the rate I was going, things were looking bleak.

The uniform ward was how I'd left it. Closet doors open, garments spilling out onto the floor. Neptune had told D'Nar that he'd take over the uniform ward duties, but he'd left it a mess. If the responsibility was still linked to me, I didn't want to leave things like they were. I located the key for the higher command level uniforms, found my size (black with gold collar and insignia) and set it on the counter next to the button that hailed the bridge. I repacked the closet. When I finished, I closed and locked the cabinet doors, and started to change.

I unzipped my magenta uniform and stepped out of it, tossing it onto the floor. I laid the black and gold uniform in front of me and undid the zipper down the back. The doors opened, and two men walked in. Too late to pull on the uniform, I grabbed it and held it up to conceal my mostly naked body.

The effort was pointless. Captain Thaddeus Swift was too much of a gentleman to comment on my inappropriate attire, and Vaan Marshall, the captain's companion, had already seen it.

14: VAAN

"Sylvia," Vaan said. He stepped toward me and I stepped back. I rearranged the uniform with my fingers and held the fabric in place like a shield.

"I was just changing," I said.

A smile toyed with Captain Swift's lips. He pointed to the doors. "We'll be right outside." They turned around and left.

Well, that was just great. I turned my back to the door and stepped into the uniform, and then reached around the back to zip it up. The fabric was thick and impervious to both heat and cold. I ran my hand over the gold insignia, and a small sound came out of it.

"Neptune," said a voice.

"You can hear me?" I asked.

"Stryker?"

"This uniform is bugged?"

"Security uniforms are fitted with radio chips so we can communicate in case of emergency," he said. "New advancement after what happened to the Moon Unit 4."

That meant it hadn't been mentioned in the outdated BOP I'd memorized. "Can I turn it off?"

"No."

"Not even at night when I'm alone in my room?"

"No."

The initial luster of being given security clearance tarnished. "I have to finish changing," I said.

"I'm not stopping you."

"How do I end this conversation?"

"Say 'Over and out.'"

"Over and out."

"Yes."

"No, I mean, I'm saying it to end the conversation."

"Okay. Over and out."

"Whatever." I was pretty sure I heard him grunt before the insignia went silent.

I stuffed my old uniform into the laundry chute on the wall and then went outside to where Captain Swift and Vaan waited.

The captain spoke. "Lt. Stryker," he said. "I came to your ward to introduce Commander Vaan Marshall to you, but I understand you two have already met."

"Yes. Commander Marshall," I said, holding out my hand.

Vaan glanced down at it, up at my face, and then back down at my hand. "Lt. Stryker," he said. He shook my outstretched hand. Like me, Vaan was Plunian. His skin tone was darker than mine but in the same neighborhood. Regardless of how I felt about having a Federation Council officer on board Moon Unit 5, after morning's encounter with the little Martians, it would be nice to not be the only purple person on the ship. Vaan's professional standing might even lend me an air of respectability by affiliation.

Vaan's hand was warm. He held onto mine a moment too long and, awkwardly, I pulled mine away. He smiled at my discomfort.

Captain Swift seemed not to notice. "Lt. Stryker, I wanted to thank you personally for your help in the engineering room last night. The two officers are recovering nicely and should be back to their posts by the end of the day. Commander Marshall will be assisting Neptune in the investigation. Give him whatever information he requires."

"Of course," I said.

"I'd like to start by interviewing you about what you saw in engineering," Vaan said.

"I'm due in security section, but let's make time to talk later today." The insignia on my uniform buzzed against me, like a tiny electrical shock. I slapped my hand over it. "Um, hold on." I lifted my hand. "Hello?" I asked.

"Give your report to the Federation Council representative. Come to Security after you're done."

"Roger that. Over and out." I looked up at the men in front of me. "I'm still figuring out how this thing works."

Captain Swift and Vaan both stifled grins. The captain spoke. "Lt. Stryker, when you and Commander Marshall finish, come join me on the bridge. I'd like to give you a tour as a thank you."

I smiled back at the captain. Take that, eavesdropping Neptune! "I'd love that," I said. I may have shifted my weight a little to make sure the insignia radio receiver on my uniform picked up my response.

Vaan followed me into the uniform ward. The soles of my boots were silent against the smooth floors. I sat on the bench along the far wall next to a locked case of gravity boots. Vaan pulled a chair up in front of me and sat down.

"Do you want me to just tell you what happened?"

"I thought we could sit and talk first. I haven't seen you in years. Not since—"

I cut him off. "Not since you people convicted my

dad."

"I recused myself from the vote against him. Federation Council made the decision, not me."

"That's right, Vaan. You recused yourself. You didn't defend him; you didn't open an investigation into the allegations against him or encourage them to review their facts. You stepped aside because you were afraid of making a stink first thing after getting appointed to the council."

"That's not fair, Syl. I'd been in the position for less than a moon cycle. It would have had long-term implications on my role within the council going forward."

"As long as you were thinking about your reputation long term, then, sure, that's fine. I totally understand your *reputation* comes before my *father*."

"I'm not here to talk about your father."

"Then why are you here? The first thing you would have done after the request came through to Federation Council was to look at the ship roster and make sure there were no conflicts of interest. You would have seen my name. Why recuse yourself back then and not now?"

"I'm here because the council was alerted to some strange activity onboard Moon Unit 5. First murder, then sabotage. Questions surround the ship's security team. I was sent to observe and make an arrest if necessary." He glanced down at my black and gold uniform. "Moon Unit security," he said. "That's what you always wanted, wasn't it? It's what you studied and trained for at the academy. It's good to see you sitting there in that uniform. It's good to see you period."

"We should get started," I said. "The council will expect you to follow procedure with a post-critical event interview. Are you ready?"

"It's been ten years, Syl. We don't have to rush anything."

"You're here to do a job, so do it." I reached forward and activated the recording device in his hand. "Preliminary interview with Lt. Sylvia Stryker aboard Moon Unit 5 as conducted by Commander Vaan Marshall. Space date: Two-twenty-three. Time: Zulu Eight." I held the wand toward him to speak or take control of the interview.

He took it from me and held his hand over the wand. "This is how you want it to be?"

"Yes."

He moved his hand from the recording device. "Lt. Stryker, why was your name only added to the security roster *after* the presence of Federation Council was requested aboard this ship?"

15: SUSPECTS

I should have expected the question. Vaan had tried to talk to me before turning on the microphone, and he'd even commented on my uniform. Back when we were in the space academy together, he'd had a leaning toward politics and I toward security. He knew what my dreams had been up to the point when the Federation Council officers arrested my dad. That's when I vowed never to become one of them. And here I was, dressed like my enemy. Neptune didn't know that. Nobody on the ship did. Except for the person sitting in front of me recording my interview for the council to judge.

"My reassignment to security was recent. I've been a member of the ship's crew since Moon Unit 5 departed."

"Your name wasn't on the roster that was submitted a month ago."

"I was a last-minute replacement for the uniform

lieutenant. And before you ask about that, the original hire had to back out of her assignment because of a broken leg. For the ship to meet its scheduled departure date, all open positions had to be filled. Since I'd already passed the background check, I was assigned to oversee the uniform ward."

"Until two days ago, your records weren't in the computer manifests."

"Ask Neptune. He's the head of Moon Unit security. He'll corroborate these facts." Neptune had to. If he told them I was lying, we'd both be taken into custody and removed from the ship. I had the benefit of knowing Neptune could hear whatever I said thanks to the communication device embedded in my new uniform. I didn't believe for a second he wasn't listening in.

Vaan seemed to find my answer suitable. "Describe what happened the night of the engineering emergency."

"Captain Swift told Neptune to check out the engineering quadrant. They suspected sabotage, and he wanted Neptune to investigate."

"Were you both on duty?"

"We were at First Dinner. The entertainment was about to start."

"Were you there on official security detail? First Dinner is for senior officers and passengers."

"We were dining."

"Together?"

"Yes."

Vaan's expression changed. I could have told him the real reason I'd been there with Neptune. I didn't. He didn't deserve it.

I'd often wondered how it would go the first time I saw Vaan after Federation Council voted to convict my dad. Now I knew. Vaan's questions were like a knife to the scar tissue of a previously broken heart. Even his attempted apology felt thin. His eyes searched my face seemingly looking for signs of the Sylvia he once knew. I couldn't let him see the vulnerability just below the surface.

"There was a vacant table and Uma Tolst, The Space Bar hostess, notified the captain," I said. Without thinking about it, my hand felt for the communication device embedded in my new uniform. "He instructed Neptune to be at dinner, and Neptune took me."

"Oh."

"It wasn't—" I cut myself off. I knew it wasn't a date and Neptune knew it wasn't a date, but there was no reason Vaan had to know that. "During dinner, Captain Swift told us about the problem. We slipped out right before the entertainment started."

"And you went to engineering. Did you have any idea what you would find when you got there?"

"Neptune said there was a problem with the computer readings, and that security protocol mandated he be there to oversee the technicians."

"Why did Neptune take you with him? If that's what the problem was, there wouldn't be a reason for a uniform lieutenant to go with him."

I wasn't about to tell Vaan that I'd been in Neptune's custody at the time. I searched for a plausible explanation that wouldn't raise additional questions. Unfortunately, there was only one thing that sprang to mind.

I sat up straighter. "I already told you. Neptune and I were at First Dinner together. Considering the circumstances, I would think you'd understand *exactly* why he didn't leave me alone. Gentlemen aren't expected to ditch their companions in the middle of an evening."

Vaan's brows dropped down over his eyes and his lips pursed together like he'd bitten into a rotten lemon. He studied me for a moment and appeared to choose his words cautiously. "How well do you know Neptune?" he finally asked. I suspected that wasn't one of his preselected questions.

"Well enough to accompany him to First Dinner."

"Neptune has a reputation in the galaxy, and it's not as a gentleman."

While I was both considerably interested in the details of Neptune's not-a-gentlemen reputation and the fact that Neptune himself was probably listening to the conversation, I fought to control my reaction. "Sometimes people aren't what they seem." I smiled a knowing smile.

Vaan looked away. I felt a wall of tension between us. That's what you get for choosing sides, Vaan Marshall. Or what you don't get. You don't get me.

"You arrived in engineering and found two men down. What happened next?"

I went on to describe the scene as we'd discovered it: the flashing red lights that cast the quadrant in an overall gray state, the sirens that made it impossible for Neptune to understand what I'd tried to tell him when I first saw the two men lying unconscious behind the computer.

"When Neptune rounded the corner and saw the men, he wanted me to help carry them out. By that time, I'd found the hose wedged in the seam between the wall panels. I felt the air on my fingertips first and then sniffed it. I knew right away what it was."

"And that was what?"

"Carbon monoxide. When we were kids on Plunia, we used to stand outside the carbon mines. Remember? It was the only place where we could escape the mostly pure oxygen that came from the ice mines. It made us dizzy—almost like how I feel when I drink too much Saturnian wine."

Vaan held his hand out as if he was about to touch me, and then he stopped and put it back onto his lap. The memory was there right below the surface. That's where we'd spent our first night together. The intoxicating combination of love, lust, and carbon monoxide had kept us out past curfew.

Vaan missed class the next day. As a result, he'd been enrolled in remedial studies and given a battery of tests to gauge his dedication to the program. I'd been grounded. The only time I was allowed to leave the mines was to attend class. And even then, I'd had a chaperone. My dad was between deliveries of ice to neighboring planets, and he shuttled me back and forth to the space academy. Those were the last memories I had of my dad before he was sent away. And in hindsight, I'd do it all again.

"So that's it. I inhaled the gas so it wouldn't spread deeper into the engineering room while Neptune got the men out."

"Lt. Stryker, for the record, what is your background?"

"My mother's family is from Earth and my dad is Plunian."

"Where were you raised?"

"Plunia."

"What made you think that you were equipped to inhale direct carbon monoxide and survive?"

"I didn't think. I just acted. The day I boarded the ship, when I found the second navigation officer dead in the uniform ward, I was too late to save him. I wasn't going to let that happen again. I saw two men passed out on the floor. I saw the hose jutting out from between two panels on the wall. I tried to get Neptune's attention, but the sirens were too loud for him to understand me. The only way to buy time for him to get them out was to stop the gas leak, so I stopped the leak."

"That's not how your mind works. You're naturally gifted at the space sciences: physics, chemistry, geometry, and trigonometry. You've had a sense of them since birth. You wouldn't just inhale a poisonous gas without first assessing the odds, knowing the risks, calculating the possible damage to you and others. You're not spontaneous like that."

I glared at him. "Don't pretend you know me,

Commander Marshall. There is more to being a member of Moon Unit 5 security team than what you read in my file." For a few long moments, we stared eye to eye. The room grew hot, and my skin felt prickly.

Neptune entered, breaking the tension. "Is this interview over? I need Stryker in security," he said.

Vaan and I stood up. Vaan switched the recording device off and said, "I hope you know what you're doing, Lt. Stryker. There's only so much I can do to protect you, and you've already willfully placed yourself way outside that zone."

16: DEBRIEFING AND A THEORY

Vaan walked past Neptune and left. I put my hands on my hips. "What do you want?"

"I want a debriefing."

"Not now. I want to get to that tour of the bridge that Captain Swift offered."

"You're not going to the bridge. Debriefing. Now."

"I thought you could hear everything I said."

"I can." He didn't look particularly thrilled.

"Then why do you need a debriefing?"

"Follow me." He turned around and left.

I looked at my surroundings. This ward was where I was supposed to be. In a small corner of the ship, away from the passengers and the security team. In charge of folding uniforms and storing them neatly between requisitions. I'd taken a big risk to get on board Moon Unit 5 in the first place, but that was because I knew I was qualified to do the job vacated by the original accident-prone uniform lieutenant as soon as I saw it listed on the ship manifest. It was a low-ranking position. It was perfect for me because I could fly under the radar.

Nobody should have had reason to question if I was qualified or how I'd passed the physical exam. Every single person on this ship had been given two uniforms before departure. The only time I'd be called on was in case of uniform infraction or promotion. The crimes on the ship had made my position far more visible than I liked.

Neptune came back in. "Stryker. Now."

I *may* have cursed at him under my breath.

I had to jog since his legs were so much longer than mine, but there was no way I was going to tell him I couldn't keep up. We went into the elevator. He swiped his card and the elevator started its descent.

"You're not putting me back in the holding cell, are you?" I asked.

"We're going to engineering."

"Why?"

"Because I want to know what you know about what happened in there."

"You do know. You just heard me dictate it to Vaan."

"Commander Marshall's line of questioning was

intended to elicit answers to a different set of questions than the ones I'm asking. And while you're working for me, you will address him—and every other ranking officer on board this ship—with the proper title."

"I can't start calling Vaan 'Commander Marshall.'"

"Unless you have evidence to strip him of his rank, then you'll show him the appropriate respect."

I almost wished I did, but I didn't. Vaan had achieved his position the hard way: through high grades and networking. Unlike the other twenty-three members of Federation Council, Vaan hadn't been born into a legacy position. A Federation Council member had died, and there had been no family line to take over. It was the kind of thing that happened only in the rarest of situations, and Vaan had been the right candidate at the right time. He was the most honest person I'd ever met. I'd tried really, really hard to hate him after he took the position, but I couldn't. That made it ten times harder to get over him. Eventually, I did.

But that didn't make us friends.

Neptune didn't ask any more questions. I sulked on my side of the elevator for the duration of our trip to engineering. Neptune acted like he always did: eyes staring forward, arms crossed, biceps flexed, mouth turned down. His lack of personality was taking all the fun out of finally having achieved a position on a security staff. I widened my own stance so my gravity boots were shoulder-width apart and crossed my arms over my chest.

"What are you doing?"

"Practicing. Isn't this the official security team pose?"

Neptune was not amused. I dropped my arms to my waist and stood in a more ladylike position. When the elevator stopped on the engineering floor, I walked out and headed toward the computer room where the gas leak had taken place. I reached the entrance and turned around. Neptune was still by the elevator.

"Aren't you coming with me?"

"No."

"Then what exactly do you want me to do?"

"Take your time. Walk around. There is no threat. I want you to absorb the scene and tell me if anything strikes you as off."

"The whole thing is off. There isn't any crew at the computer. Shouldn't somebody be making sure the ship is running in ship-shape shape?"

"I'll wait here."

I turned my back on Neptune and entered the room. As soon as I stepped onto the industrial carpeting, a chill ran over me from the inside out.

Members of the crew on the ground.

Lights flashing overhead.

Alarms sounding.

Gas leaking into the room right before I saw the hose.

I wondered, briefly, if anybody else would have felt the difference in the air quality? Or if I would have noticed it as quickly as I had if I'd been wearing my helmet?

Unless...was it possible that my helmet wasn't cracked? And that the gas leak from engineering had seeped up into the uniform ward? Where I'd found a body?

I closed my eyes and pictured the ship's schematics. The orientation packet had included a 3D rendering of Moon Unit 5, a diagram that illustrated the magnitude of the ship. The bells and whistles available to the paying passengers on their big adventure to the moons of Jupiter were on the main level, along with the bridge, Medi-bay, The Space Bar, and Ion 54, the after-hours dance club. There were other passenger-targeted entertainment options, but I wasn't concerned with them at the moment. Because when I pictured the ship, I pictured the only portion where it came together in three layers: The Space Bar, the uniform ward, and engineering. Stacked on top of each other like a sandwich.

I approached the wall where I'd found the carbon

monoxide leak. It wasn't hard to remember where I'd been when I inhaled the toxic gas. I knelt on the carpet and ran my fingers along the wall, feeling for an opening. I found it between two acoustic panels. I fed my fingers into the seam and wriggled them around. The tips of my fingers connected with the end of the tube, now recessed into the wall. I couldn't get hold of it, but I could confirm one thing. The hose was pointed down.

It had been fed into engineering from one of the floors above us. Anybody on the crew would have known where engineering was. The leak wasn't random. It had been a deliberate act to incapacitate the crew that kept the ship safely running.

I stood up and glanced around the room for anything else before leaving to give Neptune my theory. I felt a sense of unease like I was still missing something but couldn't place what. The seizure-inducing red light had been reset, and the room looked normal. Colorful buttons and switches flickered on the control panel, and the orange carpet appeared to have recently been vacuumed.

The orange carpet. No, that's not right. When did the carpet down here become orange? It was gray. I remember it being gray. The carpet was gray, and the engineering officers who had been passed out on it were in white shirts.

White. Not red.

Engineering officers wore red shirts. Just like the navigation officer. Their assigned positions could be discerned from details like the trim on their sleeves and the color of their collar. Engineering uniforms were bare bones. All about utility. The engineering officers had to be prepared for more physical tasks than other officers on the ship. It was one of the reasons their quarters were on this sublevel and not with the rest of the crew. I'd heard a rumor that Purser Frank had expressed concerns to the captain that passengers might be troubled by the appearance of men dressed in such non-glamorous garb and Captain Swift agreed. It had cost Moon Unit 5 an extra two weeks in design revisions, but the work had been done.

So why had I seen men in white uniforms on the ground?

I looked up at the ceiling. The red lights had bathed the whole room in a surreal glow. Red shirts, viewed under red light, would appear white or close to it. The orange carpet was close enough to red that the men would have all but blended in with it. Which meant I didn't know what color the men were wearing: red like engineering, or gray like flex crew.

Or both. Which meant one of the victims I'd saved

might have been faking.

17: A NEW THREAT

My observation led to a troubling theory, but it was my job to tell Neptune. I stepped into the hall.

"Can you come with me?" I asked.

"You can give your report to me now."

"It would be better if I could show you what I saw."

"That's not necessary."

Why must he be so stubborn? "Fine. The tube that dispensed the gas—"

"I know about the tube. Is that it?"

"Can you let me talk, please? Or is that asking too much?"

He—guess what?—crossed his arms over his chest. I mimicked him. I didn't care if it made him mad. I was done with subtlety. "Check the color of the shirts of the victims against the colors of the uniforms they were issued."

"Why?"

"You're a smart guy. You figure it out."

"Submit your written report by Zulu Seventeen."

"Fine." I stormed past him to the elevator, activated it, and left Neptune alone on the engineering floor while I went to my quarters.

If this was my grand peek into the world of spaceship security, then to say I was disappointed was an understatement. I'd wanted to feel responsible for the safety of the ship passengers and the crew. Keeping an eye out for malicious behavior against us. Ensuring policies were recognized, protocols were met, rules were followed.

Security was the silent leader of any ship. It garnered respect without the limelight like the captain or handful of first officers. Even Neptune, who was the head of Moon Unit security, operated in a behind-the-scenes capacity. It strengthened his position when everybody on board the ship didn't know who he was or what he did.

But this—this wasn't what I'd hoped for or expected. I'd acted like any good security officer would when discovering a threat: I'd eliminated it so the crew could be saved. And how had my immediate supervisor thanked me? He hadn't. Stupid Neptune didn't care what happened to me. He was just using me to find out what he needed to know.

Vaan said Neptune had a reputation in the galaxy. Maybe that was it. Maybe he sucked at his job. Maybe he planned to take my name off the report and put his on and take full credit for everything I'd done.

I didn't care.

I didn't care about any of it.

I didn't want to be a on board the spaceship anymore. I wanted to go home. Sure, I'd write up the report as requested. I was going to write it up, send it to Neptune, finish up the moon trek, and go back to Plunia. Employment on the Moon Unit was nothing like I'd hoped. After a lifetime of working in the mines where I'd grown up, I felt lost. Back there, I knew what I was doing. Not only that, I knew how to do it better. I'd built equipment that allowed our crew to double their output and designed fields that maximized the storage of the balls of dry ice we mined before they could be delivered to another planet. We lost a lot of business after my dad was arrested, but slowly, the existing contacts came back. It was a testament to my mother that she was able to tune out the gossip, rebuild those bridges, and keep us from losing everything.

Yes, all I had to do was write up my report, turn it over to Neptune, and wash my hands of the whole murder/sabotage thing. We were two days into the trip with only five left to go. I could handle that. I *had to* handle that. When this was all over, I'd have a story to tell the workers on Plunia who had helped my mom come up with the money to get me to the space station the day the ship deployed.

I shifted Cat from the table to the chair and opened my computer. The drive had been calibrated to analyze my voice tone and pulse and embedded those statistics into the file properties. It also transcribed the recording into a report that could be read and transferred at the push of a button. I stated my name, employee number, and rank, realized I'd said "uniform lieutenant" instead of "security officer," and wasted another fourteen minutes determining the spot on the computer hard drive to erase to match my new credentials. I reattached the motherboard and started over. All told, it took me thirty-seven minutes to finish the report. I signed off, sealed the documents, and sent them to Neptune via the ship's secure network. My job was done.

I changed out of my black security uniform into my sleep garb and stuffed the uniform into the empty trunk that I'd brought. Instead of putting the suitcase back on top of the closet, I stuck it inside and shut the door. Even if I didn't plan to make a peep for the rest of the night, there was no way I'd sleep knowing Neptune could hear me.

I pulled back the thin synthetic coverlet and climbed into my bed. As my weight hit the mattress, the lights dimmed. Cat's eyes went dark and his quiet motor whirred while he lowered himself to a sitting, and then laying position. I clicked the blue dial on the wall three settings to the right. A soft melody filtered out. The hour was late, I'd had a very long day, and it was time to go to sleep.

I closed my eyes. The memories I'd tried to keep buried all day flooded to the surface. Vaan and me sneaking off from the space academy. Vaan and me in the carbon monoxide caves on Plunia. Vaan and me lying next to each other, covered only by a blanket that had been handed down from my mother's mother to my mother and then to me, our fingers intertwined, purple against lavender. The closest I'd ever come to finding someone who made me feel like I belonged.

The door swished open, and a bright light hit me in the eyes. Cat's solar panel activated, and his eyes glowed brightly. He rolled in circles, confused by the sudden illumination.

"Stryker. Get up."

"Neptune?" I blinked repeatedly while my eyes adjusted to the light. "What are you doing in my room?

Get out! I turned in my report. I'm done." I pulled the synthetic cover over my head and rolled toward the wall.

"Your report is wrong."

I flung the coverlet back. "How could you possibly have concluded that? I sent it to you five minutes ago. If you'd bothered to check it, you'd know I wasn't lying. If I was, my report would have been red flagged after vocal analysis. It would have been forwarded to the council."

"Come with me." He turned around and walked out.

"I'm in my sleeping garb!"

He stood in the doorway with his back to me. "Come with me. Now."

I stood up and slipped my feet into my black gravity boots, and then followed Neptune into the hallway. The ship was unusually quiet. It took a moment to realize Neptune was holding a noise-cancelling device. "Hey," I said, but no sound came out of my mouth. "You can't hear me, can you?" He didn't turn around. "You sure are lucky I don't sleep in the nude."

Neptune stopped. He turned around and glared at me, his brows drawn together and his eyes narrowed. How could he possibly have heard that?

I gave him my best I-didn't-say-what-you-think-I-said look. He pointed down the hall. It didn't seem as though I had a choice about not going with him.

I reached the elevator first. At night, the halls were mostly empty, and tonight was no exception. My boots left small indentations on the carpet, but the lack of sound was eerily disturbing. Neptune activated the control panels, and we dropped down to the security level. Even if he'd turned the sound cancelling device off, the silence would have remained.

The holding cell where I'd spent the majority of yesterday sat empty. Neptune walked to the computer and pressed a few buttons. The screen lit up. He set down the noise-cancelling device, and immediately the sound of *beeps* and *boops* replaced the silence.

"You indicated in your report that the second navigation officer was responsible for the gas leak in engineering."

"That's right. He had no reason to be in the uniform ward when I arrived on the ship. There was an empty canister next to him. The uniform ward is directly above the engineering room. He must have gained access, threaded the tube into the crack in the wall, and dispensed carbon monoxide into engineering. There's a good chance one of the engineers we found passed out was in on it."

"No."

"*Yes*. Whoever killed the second nav officer likely

found him sabotaging the ship, and he died while they were trying to restrain him from finishing his actions. If we go back to the uniform ward, we might find a timer or a trip wire or something that set the gas leak off. It probably came from The Space Bar. If someone wanted to hide canisters of carbon monoxide, they could have stashed them along with the tanks of nitrous oxide that are kept there. I know Purser Frank says the nitrous oxide thing is a rumor, but I saw the crew loading the tanks when we went to dinner."

Neptune's full attention was on me while I spoke. The details were fresh in my mind since I'd just reviewed them while dictating my report. I stood silent for an awkward number of seconds before he looked away from me to the computer screen and pressed the blue button to the right. A soothing female voice spoke.

"Analysis of air quality in engineering sector indicates a high level of carbon monoxide. Tissue analysis of lungs of second navigation officer indicates inhalation of carbon monoxide. Conclusion: second navigation officer died from inhalation of carbon monoxide."

"So? He accidentally breathed in the gas leak while he was sabotaging the ship. Served him right."

Neptune hit another button on the computer. The soothing female voice spoke again. "Analysis of empty canister in uniform ward indicates tampering. Contents incorrectly marked as oxygen. Analysis of DNA on inhaler indicates second navigation officer use. Conclusion: gas leak in engineering sector and murder of second navigation officer connected."

"That can't be true. The canister that I found by the second navigation officer's body was just like the one I used after my helmet cracked."

Neptune reached next to the computer and picked up a brushed nickel tank. It was identical to the ones I kept in my room and hidden in the uniform ward. "This canister?" he asked.

"Yes."

He held it out. "Inhale."

I took the oxygen canister and pulled the pin, and then fitted the mouthpiece into my mouth and inhaled. I expected crisp, clean oxygen to fill my lungs like earlier when Doc Edison had treated me. Instead, I grew lightheaded. My lungs convulsed and my body went limp. I lost all coordination and collapsed onto Neptune's computer.

18: SPACE PIRATES

A sharp burst of oxygen exploded through me and I opened my eyes. For the third time in three days, I was inside the holding cell. Neptune knelt on the floor in front of me. He pulled his left hand away from my face and unballed his right fist. On his palm were three round white tablets.

"Oxygen pills," he said. "Take one and stay put until it releases into your system."

"You knew that canister was filled with carbon monoxide. You knew I was going to pass out."

"You weren't going to believe me just because I told you. It was faster to demonstrate."

I leaned back against the wall behind the cot. The exposed concrete was cool through my thin sleep uniform. As the oxygen transmuted into my system, the feeling slowly returned to my arms and legs. The shaking stopped. My thoughts cleared. I wasn't particularly happy about the method Neptune had used to prove to me that the navigation officer had been as much of a victim as the men in engineering, but I couldn't fault him for his reasoning. Experience was a powerful teacher. It was lesson number two at the space academy—that we would learn more from experience than from being taught. (Lesson number one was the enemy of my enemy is my friend.)

While Vaan had spent afternoons in lecture halls memorizing charts of galaxy alliances and the profiles of past members of Federation Council, I'd been sent on carefully designed tactical missions that tested my critical thinking, loyalties to my team, willingness to sacrifice others for the greater good. It was one of the reasons I'd built Cat. I wanted to know that no matter what happened in the real world, there would be someone I could talk to in the privacy of my quarters. That my confidante was a robotic cat was the subject of much ridicule once my fellow students discovered him.

"You're saying Lt. Dakkar died because—"

"Stop saying his name," Neptune interrupted. "You're violating Moon Unit protocol."

"Fine. You're saying *the second navigation officer* died because he inhaled carbon monoxide from a corrupted oxygen canister that you found in the uniform ward."

Neptune nodded once.

"That means he was as much of a victim as the engineering crew. We're not safe. The threat to the ship is still active."

Neptune nodded again.

"Then what are we waiting for? Suspicion of a standing crew member is a Code Red. We have to tell Captain Swift. He has to alert the passengers and evacuate the ship. I don't know where we are in the moon trek, but we must be approaching a space station."

"We can't stop the ship."

"Why? Because Moon Unit 5 is a cruise ship and somebody doesn't want to refund the money?"

Neptune took my hand and pulled me to my feet. He led me out of the cell, back to the computer, and this time turned the sound switch so the computer was silent. He clicked a couple of keys on the keyboard and the regulation screensaver went black. A field popped up in the middle of the screen, and he typed in his name and ID number, and then entered a string of encoded characters into ten white fields. The black screen dissolved and a news database replaced it.

"What's that?" I asked.

Neptune looked at me, his brows drawn low over his eyes. He rolled out his chair and stood, and indicated that I should sit. Curious about this sudden change in Neptune and his willingness to share information with me, I dropped onto the molded plastic and leaned forward to read the screen.

Bulletins appeared character by character on the bottom as if someone at a remote location was typing them while events were unfolding. As new information appeared on the bottom of the screen, the existing news scrolled up and the bulletins on the top disappeared.

Space Pirates from Colony 13 have infiltrated the galaxy. Safe zones compromised.

I immediately understood why we couldn't make an unscheduled stop. Pirates were the biggest threat to the galaxy. They operated by their own code, one that made allowances for murder, torture, theft, and kidnapping if those actions got them what they wanted. They were the same people my father had been accused of colluding with to maximize the value of our ice mine yield.

Nobody wanted to believe that Jack Stryker had been capable of entering a deal with pirates, but the evidence had been incontrovertible. Worse, he hadn't denied the accusations. My dad had remained silent when the Space Police Corps came to the mine and arrested him and through his trial at the Federation Council. Whether or not he was talking now, I wouldn't know. I'd never know as long as I stayed away from Colony 13.

I read what I could from the news monitor, picking out enough words to understand the magnitude of the threat. As long as we were on Moon Unit 5, we were safe. Once we stopped, we'd be a prime target. Which meant the devil we knew—the on-ship murderer and saboteur—was better than the devil we didn't know—the violent and unscrupulous space pirates on a rampage through the galaxy.

Neptune switched the monitor to black.

"Hey!" I said. "I was reading that."

"You read enough. We need a plan."

"Here's my plan. I'm going back to bed. Tomorrow morning, I'll get up early so I can beat the Martians to the cafeteria. I'll get my food to go and eat it in my room. When we land on Ganymede, I'll request a transfer and take a space taxi back to Plunia."

"You're not going back to Plunia." Neptune's face was rigid.

I didn't care if he didn't like my attitude. At the moment I didn't much like his. "Oh, yes I am. I want off this ship. You can find yourself another helper."

"Did you not read the news? Those pirates are

tearing up the galaxy. Any attempt to land will put the safety of every passenger on this ship in danger. If conditions don't improve, we're not going to land on Ganymede. We're not going to land anywhere. You're stuck on this ship whether you like it or not."

"We have to land eventually. There's only enough fuel on board to keep us in orbit for two weeks."

"Which means we don't have to worry about that problem yet. Right now, the only problem we have is figuring out who's sabotaging the ship."

I stood up. "Are you kidding? That might be *your* only problem, but it's not mine. My coworkers want to lynch me. I haven't had a proper night of sleep in two days. My ex-boyfriend has me under surveillance, my old boss wants me written up for a wardrobe infraction, and my new boss just poisoned me with carbon monoxide. If somebody doesn't kill me because I know too much about the murder, I'm going to die in a space crash when Moon Unit 5 runs out of fuel. This trip was supposed to be my dream, and now all I want is to go home. I want to go back to work in the ice mines on Plunia. I want to go where I'm wanted. I want to be with my mom."

Neptune's expression changed. He switched the monitor back on and clicked a small green tab on the bottom that said *Plunian News*. A pop-up window filled the screen. Neptune pulled his chair away from the desk so I could get a better look at the article, but as soon as I made out the headline, I hated him for keeping it from me in the first place, and I hated him for showing it to me now.

Pirate Attack Destroys Dwarf Planet

Images of my home planet taken from a remote camera that monitored the galaxy filled the screen. Plunia exploding. Particles dispersing. My home planet dissolving into black nothingness.

The only world I knew was gone.

I looked away. Neptune put his hand under my jaw and turned my face back to the screen. I stared at the destruction of my planet, hating him for making me watch what I was bound to replay in future nightmares. I tried to turn my head, but Neptune's hand kept my face pointed toward the news bulletins. It was only then that I noticed the bottom screen crawl.

Pirates Kill Ice Mine Owner

To the rest of the galaxy, the loss of critical dry ice supplies would take precedence over the smaller story running along the bottom of the screen. But to me, it was all that mattered. Because everything I'd wanted—my hopes, my dreams, my opportunities—had come to me because of my mother's sacrifices. When our lives had been torn apart, she'd made a new future for us. And now she'd been killed at the hands of the very men who had corrupted my dad.

19: ALONE

I shouldn't have taken the job on this ship. I should have been back where I belonged, on Plunia, helping with the family business. I should have been there to help my mom fight off the attack and maybe save her life. But instead, I was here, chasing dreams that should have died a long time ago and pretending to be something I wasn't.

I didn't want to read the article. Not while Neptune was sitting in the chair next to me, studying my reaction. My life had been destroyed once thanks to space pirates. And now, they'd taken the one person who had gotten me through those troubling times. If pirates were onboard Moon Unit 5, I had no doubt I would kill them. My lifetime desire to work in security and the newfound credentials that made me look official were worth nothing.

Nothing.

"She wouldn't have wanted you to give up this opportunity to be there with her," Neptune said.

"You don't know anything about my mother, and you don't know anything about me." My voice was detached and emotionless. I felt cold. I stood up straight and stared ahead, focusing on the wall at the end of the hallway. "Are we done here?"

"Stryker," Neptune said. He put his hand on my arm. I looked down at it for a few seconds and then stepped away from him. The distance forced his hand to fall from my skin. I clenched my jaw so hard my teeth ground together. There was nothing inside of me. Not sadness, not anger, not fear. Just a black hole. I was alone now, alone in the universe with nobody on my side.

"Am I spending the night here or in my quarters?" I asked.

"You can go to your quarters."

I nodded once and then turned around and left. My movements felt robotic, as though I'd been programmed to move the same way I'd programmed Cat. I must have activated the elevator and traveled the hallway to my door, but I didn't remember doing any of it. I went inside and crawled under the temperature-sensitive blanket. I was cold. So cold. I curled up on my side with my knees up to my chest and my arms folded in front of me. My entire body shook with chills.

The temperature-sensitive blanket must have malfunctioned. Nothing I did made me warm. I stared at the wall in front of me. I didn't want to close my eyes or fall asleep. I didn't want to let time move forward. If I could stay awake, in the privacy of my room, I could pretend everything was the way it had been when I left Plunia.

***

I don't know when sleep won the coin toss, but I woke the next morning to the sound of Cat meowing my alarm. I was roasting under several temperature-sensitive blankets and a pile of clothes. I pushed the layers off me and then yelled when I saw I had company.

Pika sat at my table. Her pointy ears jutted up on either side of her head, and her eyes were twice the size they'd been the day before.

I stared at her for a moment, not saying a word. At first, I just felt sleepy, like I'd taken medication that had left me groggy. The pile of clothes on top of me and the presence of Pika didn't make sense.

And then, the horror came back to me. The news article about the space pirates. The destruction of Plunia. The death of my mother.

The sense of being completely alone.

I brushed at my shoulders, feeling like one of the heat-sensitive blankets was still there. It wasn't. The weight was imaginary. I felt like I had the day my dad had been arrested and taken to Colony 13, only worse. Everyone would watch me, judge me, pity me. Somehow I had to find an inner strength to carry me beyond the gossip and criticism of the crew members and passengers and anybody else I'd encounter for the rest of my life. I had to turn off my emotions and use my Plunian mind to focus on facts: cold, hard facts. The opposite of emotion.

Fact: Two plus two equals four.

Fact: Red and yellow make orange.

Fact: People can't be trusted.

I shifted my gaze from Pika to the mound of clothes piled on my bed. They were crew uniforms. "Why are there uniforms on my bed?" I asked.

"You were cold, and the temperature blankets weren't warming you."

"The blankets are standard issue. I only had one. Where did the rest come from?"

"I took one from the second navigation officer's room." Pika smiled a little. "Nobody thought to check his quarters after he died. That's where I've been staying."

Again, I wondered if I'd been foolishly accepting

Pika's innocent act. She knew her way around the ship without being noticed. She was smart enough to hole up in the quarters vacated by the deceased officer. But now, I didn't care. Let someone else figure out what happened. I doubted anybody was going to risk their life trying to find out what happened to my mother.

"That explains one extra blanket, but not two. And since you're a stowaway, you can't tell me the third one is yours."

"It belongs to the giant."

"You stole Neptune's blanket?"

"He gave it to me."

I pushed the pile of gray uniforms to the floor and peeled off the top blanket. "Take it back," I said. "I don't need Neptune's charity."

As I held the blanket out toward Pika, I realized the pink alien was shivering. I didn't know how she'd gotten into my quarters or the uniform ward that first day on the ship. I didn't ask. She'd already demonstrated that she was able to get into places she probably shouldn't have been. I walked across the room and draped the extra blanket over her narrow shoulders. The cloth immediately turned a soft orange shade as it adjusted to her Gremlon temperature. Her fists grabbed at the edges, and she wrapped it tight around her body. "Thank you," she said in a little girl voice.

"You're welcome."

I picked up the uniform closest to me and started folding. It was a mindless task, the least important one I could choose. I needed something that required no thought. Hold the shirt to my chest. Fold each sleeve in: left one first and right one next. Raise the hem of the shirt to the shoulders so the shirt was folded over itself. Set it on the pile and move onto the next one. Neither Pika nor I spoke while I worked my way through the pile. When I finished, I had twelve gray tops and sixteen pairs of black trousers. I moved the piles from the bed to the table.

"Did you get any sleep last night?" I asked Pika.

She watched me with wide eyes but didn't answer. I tipped my head toward the bed. "Go ahead and lay down. Nobody is going to come looking for you here either."

"Where are you going?"

"I have to return these uniforms to the inventory closet before anybody notices they're missing."

"Wait," Pika said. She extended her closed fist out from under the blanket. "I'm not allowed to let you leave without these."

I felt my forehead scrunch in confusion and held my hand out. Pika turned her fist sideways and opened her fingers. Three round white pills fell into my palm. Only one person had offered me oxygen tablets since being on board the ship. Only one person knew my oxygen canisters had been tampered with and filled with carbon monoxide. One person knew everything I knew: about what I'd figured out in engineering and what had happened to my home planet. One person who controlled my future.

"Pika, what can you tell me about the giant?"

Pika's eyes widened. "I'm not allowed to talk about him."

"He gave you these pills, didn't he? He told you to come into my room and watch over me. Why? Does he know you're a stowaway? Why is he okay with you being on the ship?"

Pika's ears popped out on top of her head, and her body mass diminished. I hadn't known Gremlons could change size at will, and I leaned forward to study her. "How'd you do that?"

"I didn't do anything. I didn't do anything. I didn't do anything."

"You got smaller."

"No, I didn't."

"Yes, you did."

"No, I didn't."

"I saw you. Your ears popped up, and your body

shrank. Why? And how?"

Slowly Pika's ears retracted closer to her head. She pulled the heat-adjusting thermal blanket up to her neck. "The giant told me you were sick and I should give you those when you woke up so you could get better."

"How did you get in here?"

"He let me in."

"Neptune was in my room *again?*"

Pika's looked scared. "He was worried about you. He said you were aloner than anybody else on the ship."

I didn't correct Pika or ask to hear the exact words Neptune had used because it didn't matter. I *was* alone. In a ship of passengers who were having the time of their lives, I was without a single person I could trust.

20: LASHING OUT

I changed into my black security uniform, picked up the stacks of uniforms, and left Pika behind in my quarters. I felt nothing. No enthusiasm for being on the ship, no pride in a job well done, no determination to prove I belonged. I was empty.

Two of the little green men who had confronted me yesterday morning passed me in the hallway. I kept my eyes forward and my gravity boots walking one foot in front of the other. Their voices floated to me from behind. "First one Plunian, now two. What's next? Little purple babies?"

"That one seems like a real handful. Bet that's why her dad took off with space pirates and screwed over their whole planet. Worthless trash."

I dropped the uniforms in the hall, a dark gray pile on top of the orange industrial carpet. I turned around and watched the Martians as they walked away, totally unaware that I'd overheard them. Or maybe they were aware. Maybe they'd wanted me to hear. Maybe this was how life was going to be from now on.

Rage burned like a supernova. I ran toward the Martians. The carpet silenced my footsteps, and by the time they realized I was right behind them, I had jumped on the back of one and knocked him to the ground. He writhed underneath me, but I was bigger, stronger, and madder than he was. I was too far gone to stop or realize what I was doing. I slapped at him, pummeled him, and a strange scream I never knew I could make came from my throat.

The other man tried to pull me off. I flung him away. He staggered backward and stumbled into the wall. He regained his footing and took off down the hall.

The man beneath me cowered and held up his arms. "Don't hurt me!" he cried out.

"Take it back! My mother was not trash!" I yelled.

"I take it back! I take it all back! Stop hitting me!"

The only fighting I knew was what they'd taught us at the space academy in Security Section Maneuvers. They were defensive moves, not offensive ones. But there was no way to pretend my assault on the communication officer in the hallway was anything other than offensive.

Unless someone had overheard what they'd said.

Two strong tawny arms wrapped themselves around me from behind and lifted me off the little green man. I was in the air. I raised my legs and made contact with the wall and pushed off as hard as I could. The arms tightened around me, and I felt like I was in a compressor.

"Get ahold of yourself," said a voice in my ear.

The mass behind me was Neptune. How did he know—oh. The chip in the security uniform.

A wave of unwanted heat washed over me. It was so strong I knew without looking that my skin color had intensified. Neptune was the one person on this ship who knew why I was angry. And somehow, that knowledge was like a release valve for my rage. My legs went limp against the wall and, because he was applying a counter pressure, I got squished. He must have realized the fight had left me because he took a step back and held on until my feet found the ground. I expected him to let go of me, but he didn't. Not right away.

The two of us stood facing the wall. I didn't want to make eye contact with him, or the Martian on the ground, or the other Moon Unit 5 crew that had come out of their quarters and the employee lounge to see who was making all the ruckus. I looked up at the lights on the top of the hallway. They were flashing white; two flashes close together. Code White: general crew disturbance. Protocol: evacuate quadrant.

The elevator doors slid open, and a team of medical officers got off. Doc Edison was in front. The expression on his face wasn't as understanding as it had been yesterday when he'd given me a sugar pop in the holding cell.

Doc and his team moved past me and assessed the officer on the ground. He was sitting up and scowling at me. I looked away, only to see Captain Swift heading down the hallway toward us.

"Do what I say," Neptune said quietly.

I turned my head ever so slightly toward him. "I still don't know if I trust you."

"I accept that." Without missing a beat, he continued. "Request a private audience. Do not apologize. It is your only acceptable course of action." He dropped his arms and took a step backward.

"Captain Swift, may I request a private audience to discuss my actions here?" I said. I hated doing what Neptune instructed me to do, but I didn't have any better ideas.

The Martian's eyes nearly bugged out of his head, which made the request worth it. Captain Swift's expression remained completely unreadable. I suspected that came in handy when he was forced to deal with unpleasantries like this. He raised his radio to his lips. "Yeoman D'Nar, your charge, Lt. Sylvia Stryker, has just requested a private audience in Council Chambers."

Her voice came back pinched and whiny. "Lt. Stryker has done nothing but violate protocol since this ship departed."

"Meet us in Council Chambers, Yeoman. We'll discuss Lt. Stryker's behavior there."

"I will not be held accountable for her actions," Yeoman D'Nar said.

"Act professionally, Yeoman D'Nar," Captain Swift admonished. I wished I could see the expression on her face.

Neptune did his arm-crossing thing. "For reasons that will become evident when we convene in Council Chamber, I will accompany you."

I'd spent most of my time on Moon Unit 5 in the uniform ward, the holding cell, and my quarters. The time I spent in engineering had a hallucinogenic cloud cast over it thanks to the gas leak, and even the brief time spent at The Space Bar had faded to a memory I wasn't certain I hadn't dreamed up. But even though I hadn't been through the main corridors of the ship, I had studied it so thoroughly that I didn't hesitate. I still had adrenaline to burn, and if Captain and Neptune couldn't keep up, that was their problem.

Council Chambers was a soundproof and magnetically sealed meeting space located at the front of the Moon Unit. Every one of the four preceding Moon Units had had them—well, I still didn't know for sure about the Moon Unit 4, but I assumed it had met the same overall requirements of the previous three. The room was intended for confidential discussions of intergalactic importance. I was humbled to know that my behavior had put me into that category.

I led the procession in the direction I knew to be correct. The assorted crew members who had appeared after my attack on the Martians had returned to their quarters as was protocol when the flashing lights were active. That's when it hit me. *I* was the risk. I didn't want or need a private audience with Council Chambers, but it was too late.

Neptune had a master plan. Too bad I had no idea what it entailed.

21: COUNCIL CHAMBERS

Council Chambers was a sleek room that housed an oblong table and chairs. Each seat around the table had a small black stand in front of it. One by one, senior officers of Moon Unit 5 arrived. Each stopped by a computer library on the left side of the room and withdrew a tablet from its port, and then sat around the table and connected to an alternate power source. Screens glowed one at a time with an orange background and the Moon Unit insignia in the center in black and white. Two moons circled a planet in an off-center arc that mirrored our current trek to Ganymede.

I didn't know how long it took for the senior crew to arrive at Council Chambers, but the BOP indicated that when a Code White—or subordinate crew member threat—was identified, the second officers were to take over first officer posts so the problem could be addressed immediately. When the six attendees—five plus Vaan—had arrived, the door swished shut and a barrier slid down from ceiling to floor to isolate the panels that allowed them to open. We were here, and we were going to stay here, until the issue resolved.

Now that we were all gathered in the room, I wasn't sure what to expect. There'd been nothing in the BOP about a private audience—probably because the only people who would be requesting private audiences were those who had committed some frowned upon infraction.

I leaned closer to Neptune. "What happens now?"

He raised an eyebrow. "I thought you knew."

I shook my head.

"Once everyone is seated and signed in, you address the council and tell them what happened."

This time *I* raised an eyebrow. "The truth, Stryker. All anybody wants to hear from you is the truth."

Whether I wanted to acknowledge the circumstances that had led to me holding court in Council Chambers or not, I knew telling the truth was the only way. The first course at space academy security training had included over fifty ways to identify if someone was lying. The course culminated in a timed test and those who couldn't recognize all fifty-seven body language and verbal tells in under a minute were expelled from the academy. My class had started with ninety-six members. That single course had whittled us down to fewer than twenty.

I'd set a new record for how quickly anyone had recognized all of the signs: seventeen seconds. Vaan and I had celebrated with a bottle of Saturnian wine I'd swiped from my dad's secret stash.

I stood stoically while the officers carried their computer to their seats, connected them, and then held their palm against the orange screen to scan in their identities. When the last of the officers had completed the task, Captain Swift turned to me.

"Lt. Stryker, you requested this assembly, so let's get right to it. State your name and rank for the record."

I moved to the end of the table and looked at the officers seated around the room. "Lt. Sylvia Stryker, security section aboard Moon Unit 5."

Yeoman D'Nar cleared her throat loudly. A few heads turned her direction. "Unless I'm mistaken, the uniform ward is not part of security section," she said.

Neptune stood. "Lt. Stryker's educational background is in security. We have an active threat on board this ship. As the ship's senior security officer and private counsel to Captain Swift, I reassigned Lt. Stryker to my team."

"You can't do that!" D'Nar said. "Not without consulting with me. She is *my* responsibility. People expect her to be in the uniform ward where she belongs, not running around the ship attacking other officers."

I fought to control my temper. The ensuing tension broke when Vaan responded. "Lt. Stryker was in the top of her class at the space academy. She is more qualified to work security on this ship than the next ten candidates on the waitlist. Neptune is correct. There is a threat on board this ship, and the number one priority is for that threat to be contained. To do that, he needs the best staff he can get."

It surprised me to hear Vaan speak up on my behalf, but I knew any friction between the yeoman and Neptune would have escalated if not for the interference of the stranger from Federation Council. Vaan knew of my accomplishments, not because he'd had a hand in getting me where I was, but because of our past. Yeoman D'Nar didn't need to know that too.

I stepped a half step forward and reclaimed the floor. "As you can see, Yeoman, I am dressed in the approved uniform for Moon Unit 5 security. I made no secret of my reassignment. My actions in the hallway were mine alone and were a manifestation of my grief over the destruction of my home planet, Plunia, and the death of my mother at the hands of space pirates, two facts that I learned of less than twenty-four hours ago. I will accept whatever punishment the council deems appropriate."

I bowed my head. The words coming out of my mouth felt clunky and mechanical. They weren't mine. But just like the rules of the ship that I'd memorized from the BOP I'd bought on the black market, I'd learned those lines from my dog-eared copy of *The Rules and Regulations for Working Aboard a Moon Unit vol. 3.*

I'd rewritten the words in the margins of the manual, crossing off what didn't apply to me and making substitutions that fit my circumstances. I'd memorized it just in case. And now, the speech tumbled out as if on autopilot.

I peeked up and looked around the room at the various expressions to gauge their reactions. What I saw were six faces staring at screens in front of them: Captain Swift, Yeoman D'Nar, Vaan Marshall, Purser Frank, Doc Edison, and Neptune. The bright reflection of blue, and then white flashed across each of them, casting their skin in unnatural shades. I shifted my weight slightly so I could see on a nearby screen what had their attention. It took me a moment before I realized they were watching footage of the cataclysmic destruction Plunia.

Neptune had tried to keep me from seeing that footage last night. But he must have known they'd show it here behind closed doors.

And then it hit me. Neptune hadn't been looking out for me when he suggested I take this course of action. He was after something else and was using me and my situation to get it. I shifted my attention from the screens to him. He was watching me. When our eyes connected, his lips pressed together into a narrow line. He cut his eyes to the group and back to me, and then did it again. He was trying to tell me something. What? What could he possibly want me to see in the faces of the officers assembled in the room?

I looked back at the group. The screens had powered off, and they were watching me as if expecting me to address them again. Only this time, the expressions were different. This time, I saw pity.

I *hated* pity.

"Captain Swift, I take full responsibility for my actions in the hallway today. The crew members I attacked were merely an outlet for my anger. I recognize that punishment can include my immediate expulsion from Moon Unit 5. If that is your decision, I won't challenge it."

I felt, rather than saw two physical reactions: Vaan and Neptune. Yeoman D'Nar narrowed her eyes at me, and I knew if it had been up to her, I would have been dematerialized and then rematerialized elsewhere before the group left the confines of the room. What she hadn't anticipated was that I wasn't yet done making my statement.

"However, before making that decision, I would like you to review my actions on the ship prior to learning news of my home planet."

Neptune stepped forward. "May I recommend Lt. Stryker be placed on probation and in my custody for the duration of the trip? I believe she will be of value to me in my investigation. I will take responsibility for her."

He was like a broken record!

I was already in custody. Or I had been. My magnetic bracelet had only just come off, and Neptune was getting permission to put it back on. Never mind the integrated recording device in my uniform that allowed him to hear everything I said. If someone had given me the option, I very well might have chosen dematerialization myself.

Captain Swift stood and addressed me directly. "Lt. Stryker, allow me to express my deepest condolences on the death of your mother and the destruction of your planet. Your actions today were not in adherence with the accepted conducts of a Moon Unit officer, so while I think we can all understand your behavior, we cannot condone it with the reward of special assignment. You will finish out the duration of the moon trek as the uniform supervisor, lieutenant, second rank, reporting to Yeoman D'Nar. When we return to the space station, you will be turned over to Federation Council for an insubordination hearing."

I pulled myself up to my tallest height and stared straight ahead so I would not have to see the smirk I assumed was on Yeoman D'Nar's face. The captain addressed the others in the room. "So as not to raise any concern amongst our paying passengers, this sentence is to remain confidential. Doc, carry out the security procedure."

"You can't mean that," Doc Edison said. His face showed open disbelief. "This girl saved two engineers. If she hadn't identified that gas leak in engineering, this whole ship would have turned into a fireball. She's a hero. We can't chip her."

Chip me? What did he mean? My brain spun like a super computer trying to make a match between star charts in two separate galaxies. Before I came up with an answer, Vaan stood.

"I agree with the doctor. You can't chip her. She's part Plunian. She has no planet to return to after this. If she tries to live anywhere on the M-13, she'll be held to the 90% compliance."

That's when the horrifying reality of what Captain

Swift suggested fully dawned on me and I realized, no matter how bleak my future had seemed last night, if I were chipped, it would be worse.

The M-13 was a stretch of the galaxy that adhered to a strict ninety percent compliance on resident profiles. It was where outcasts and criminals went when they reformed and wanted to start a new life, for one reason. Ninety percent of the people on the planets within the M-13 jurisdiction of space had been profiled and chipped, so their whereabouts were always known. They sacrificed privacy for technology. Everything about them was public: their ID, bank info, criminal pasts, marital and medical status...all were housed in open computer files available for anyone to access. The crime rate in M-13 was low but not nonexistent. The ten percent that weren't cataloged were blamed for most of the crimes, but it was more likely that somebody had found a way to buck the system.

The M-13 was under the military enforcement of Federation Council. The same Federation Council that had convicted my father. And now, the captain had issued an order for me to be chipped. Everything about me would be made public in the system. *Like father, like daughter.* That's what everyone would say.

Only then did I realize that nobody in the room could stop what was about to happen. Captain Swift had issued a direct order for Doc Edison to shoot a microscopic tracking chip into the back of my neck. I'd be branded a criminal for the rest of my life.

I looked around the room, only just now fully realizing the risk I'd taken by hacking into the computer to be here. How I'd been driven by dreams and goals and a desire to cut all ties with my criminal dad to the point that I'd committed my own crime and was about to lose my freedom.

For the first time in my life, I felt real fear. But no matter what I felt, no matter how much I'd learned about the inner workings of this ship and the backgrounds of the staff, no matter how off the charts I was regarding outcome assessment and strategic positioning, I never could have predicted what happened next.

22: CHIPPED

Doc Edison made it clear that he didn't agree with the decision to chip me. Apparently, that didn't matter. In a move faster than I expected someone with Neptune's build to be able to make, the senior security officer snatched the chipping gun from Doc, pivoted, and jabbed the barrel into the base of my skull. I felt the cold metal pressed into my hot skin, and then heard *kachung*. A prick of heat shot into the back of my neck. A split second later, I felt the chill I'd heard described as ice flooding through my veins. Having been raised on an ice farm, I had often questioned the possible accuracy of that description.

It was spot-on.

Neptune slammed the chip gun onto the table. "Lt. Stryker will report to uniform ward management at Zulu Five."

No one had acknowledged it, but Vaan had lost his home planet too. Relationship baggage notwithstanding, right now, we were the closest thing each other had to an ally on this ship.

As the sensation of ice flooded my system, my limbs felt sluggish and hard to maneuver. Whatever Vaan might have been thinking, it didn't involve snatching me from Neptune's grasp, running out of the chamber meeting, and submerging me in hot, hot water. He seemed paralyzed by torn loyalties. I knew there wasn't much he could have done, if anything, but still. He chose his side, and it was political. The very last thing I saw was the horror on Vaan's face.

Neptune picked me up, one arm under the back of my neck and one under my bent knees. I felt dizzy and went limp against him. I wanted to fight but couldn't. My limbs shook. I pulled my arms up against my chest for warmth. The room filled with judgment. I closed my eyes so I didn't have to see it.

Sounds from the room came at me as if through a tunnel, and I had a hard time making out who said what. Someone called Neptune an idiot—was that Doc?—, laughter, and whispers. And then silence.

The doors opened, and I felt myself jostle against Neptune's chest. I fought against the cloud in my brain.

Now was not the time to let injected chemicals interfere with my deductive reasoning. I had to focus on one detail, one tiny detail, and once I could make sense of that, the rest of the world could come into focus too.

I opened my eyes. The side of my head rested against the logo on Neptune's uniform. The logo was where the integrated recording device was in my uniform. It must have been the same for him. I took a deep breath and whispered into his chest, "I can't believe you chipped me. I thought we were on the same side." The effort of speaking took more energy than I'd expected.

"Don't talk," Neptune said. "Relax."

I forced my eyes open and looked up at his face. From my angle, all I got was the bottom of his chin. "No," I said. "I'm not doing what you say anymore."

"Okay, then talk. Tell me who you think killed Dakkar."

"Don't say his name. He's not a person, remember? His identity is his rank, just like me. I'm not the daughter of Jack Stryker, I'm the uniform lieutenant aboard Moon Unit 5."

"Tell me about your father. Tell me what happened."

"Don't try to trick me," I said. And then images filtered into my brain. Faces appeared and disappeared like partially materialized aliens who changed their minds about where they wanted to land. "Vaan," I said.

"Don't talk to me about Vaan," Neptune said.

"But I want to talk about Vaan. I have to talk about Vaan. He's just like me."

"He's nothing like you."

"He's just like me only he's not at all." I felt like what I was trying to say and what I was saying weren't matching up.

Neptune carried me through the halls of ship until we reached the staff quarters. "Hold out your hand," Neptune said.

"No." I balled my fist. Sure, he was strong, but he was going to have to wrestle my palm open before I'd help him.

"Name the fifty-seven verity tells."

"I don't want to."

"Number one: eye contact. Number two: shallow breathing. Number three: perspiration."

"If you already know them, why do you need me to tell you?" I asked. He wasn't making any sense.

"You need to focus on something you know until your brain clears."

So, I focused on one thing: my anger. The cloud of confusion dissipated from my thoughts. Anger filled me, fueled me, and I struggled against Neptune's arms.

"You don't care about me. You shot a subcutaneous tracking chip into the base of my skull. I'm half earthling, you moron! Did you stop for a second to consider the long-term ramifications of messing with my spinal cortex? And what that chip would do to my cognitive functions? That's what I got, Neptune. When the powers that be were handing out skill sets, I got a brain. You destroyed that without a second thought."

My body drained of the exerted energy of telling Neptune off, and I felt myself deflating. I looked away from him. "Why did you have to chip me? I was starting to like you. Now I can't like you anymore."

Neptune hesitated for a moment. "I did what I did for your safety."

I tipped my head forward, and my hair fell to either side of my face. I pressed my fingers against the back of my neck where Neptune had pressed the muzzle of the gun.

I grabbed his hand and made him feel where he'd shot the chip. "You hurt me. I want you to feel where you hurt me."

My hand was on top of Neptune's, and I pressed his fingers into my flesh. I expected it to hurt, but it didn't. Unlike the icy cold of the tracking chip, his fingertips were warm. His thumb and forefinger glided across my skin in a rhythmic manner, hypnotizing me and making me forget about what had taken place.

"Relax, Stryker. Everything will be okay."

"No, it won't. It'll never be okay again. You ruined me."

He was quiet for a moment. And then, "You're due in the uniform ward in the morning." He grabbed my wrist and pried my hand open, and then waved it in front of the door. I was tired and confused and a little sick. I stumbled into my quarters and landed on my bed. Whatever was going to happen to me now was anybody's guess.

23: DISCOVERING THE TRUTH

I woke with a headache that rivaled the one I'd had after drinking bootleg liquor from the chem lab at the space academy. It felt like someone had stapled my head to the carpet. I tried to sit up twice before realizing my head was, indeed, now attached to my bed. I reached up to free my hair when a pillow came down over my face.

"Stop it stop it stop it!" said Pika's soft voice. The pillow raised off me, and her pale pink face peeked over the top of it. "I'll untie your hair, but you have to be still."

"Why is my hair tied?"

Pika set the pillow aside and used her long skinny fingers to untangle my hair. I had no idea what she'd done to me, but unless I wanted to be bald like Vaan, I needed my hair.

"The giant told me to make sure you were safe. He said to make sure you put on your sleep uniform and to watch you all night. But you got boring, and I wanted to play with your cat, so I had to make sure you couldn't get away."

I looked down at my thermal pajamas. I only vaguely remembered changing into them and shoving my security uniform in the closet. I didn't remember Pika being in the room when I'd gone to sleep.

"Pika, what is my hair tied to?"

"The aluminum bed frame." She continued working. I couldn't see the damage, and I didn't know exactly how she'd done whatever she'd done, but the length of time it took her to work indicated she'd entertained herself with securing me before allowing herself to play with Cat. When she finished, she stood back and smiled widely, showing off all fifty of her teeth. It was a little creepy, to tell you the truth.

I sat up. "Okay, good. Now, I'm going to need your help getting off the ship. What is this, the fifth day of the trip? We should dock this afternoon. That's going to have to work." I thought about the ship's trek to Jupiter's largest moon, how Purser Frank had talked about the half day of sightseeing on Ganymede's vacation space station during our walk back to my quarters after I'd inhaled the gas in Engineering, and what I would need to survive on the space station once I escaped the Moon Unit. "I'll make a list of what I'll need. Will you help me get them? I'll need supplies. Maps. Oxygen tablets. And a distraction. I'm *definitely* going to need a distraction."

Pika picked up the pillow again and held it in front of her. "You can't escape the ship! You're my friend."

"You can come with me," I said.

"No, I can't. I belong to—I can't."

"Pika, how did you get on the ship?"

"I can't tell you."

"Can't or won't?"

"We don't have time. The giant is waiting for you in the uniform ward."

"You're right. I have to act like everything is normal and make a plan. We'll talk about this after my shift ends."

I dug my black security uniform out from my suitcase and changed into it. I'd trade it for a fresh magenta one to fit my new rank—my original rank—when I got to the uniform ward. I secured an oxygen canister to my thigh, and ran the tube underneath the fabric and out the collar. When that was done, I snapped on my bubble helmet. I no longer cared if the bubble made me stand out in a one-of-these-things-is-not-like-the-others way. This ship was teeming with bullies, criminals, and little green men. If they saw *me* as the freak, then so be it.

The hallways were empty. I arrived at the uniform ward and scanned myself in. It was as I'd last seen it: the BOP sitting out on the counter. My sleeve, torn from my original uniform, jutting out from under the bench where I'd sat and talked to Vaan. The only differences were the pile of uniforms that had been dumped on the floor and the presence of Neptune leaning on the far wall with his massive arms crossed in front of his fitted black T-shirt.

A rush of emotions washed over me. Anger. Annoyance. Anxiety.

Fear.

I tried to dismiss that one too, but it overwhelmed me like a balloon that expanded into the room. I double-tapped the valve on my oxygen canister to regulate my breathing.

"Stryker," Neptune said. "How are you feeling this morning?"

"Why do you care?" I watched him for a long moment, not sure if I even wanted to hear his answer.

He glanced down at my black uniform. "I didn't expect you to wear that today."

"I'll change as soon as you leave me alone. You can come back after hours and take this one back to your lair."

Neptune stood like a wall in front of me, not even giving me the satisfaction of a flinch at my insult. "One of the people from the council chamber session is the murderer. I needed a reason to get them all into the same room so I could observe them. You gave me that reason."

"You used me? As bait? Is there no limit to the actions you'll take or the people you'll use?"

He stood up, away from the wall, and repositioned his feet to shoulder width apart. He stared me directly in the face. "What did you learn at the space academy about assessing the enemy?"

"Why? Are you trying to figure out my next move?"

"I'm not the enemy."

"Every time I start to believe that you hurt me."

Neptune's normally chiseled-in-stone features softened. His eyes held mine, and for the first time since being on the ship, I stared back into their deep, almost black depth. Neptune knew more about me than anybody else on the Moon Unit, and in that moment, even though I knew nothing of his past, I felt like I was looking in a mirror. "Answer the question," he said gently.

Enemy Assessment was an advanced course at the space academy. I'd looked forward to it from the moment I'd enrolled. The class was taught by a commander from the intergalactic space army whose identity was secret. The trouble with my dad had taken place that same semester, and I'd had to drop out of class and return to

Plunia to help my mother with the ice mines. After I'd left, there'd been some scuttlebutt about the faculty, and Enemy Assessment had been replaced with code-breaking.

I tried not to think about the opportunities lost after I'd dropped out of my schooling, but missing the chance to have been taught that course by that professor haunted me. Enemy assessment learned from a textbook wasn't the same. Unfortunately, my book knowledge of the subject was the only knowledge I currently had.

"Identify potential enemies. Assemble them in an isolated environment. Create a situation that requires a decision. Assess individual reactions to find the one that doesn't fit protocol. That's the one who has the most to lose."

"That's what I did. What we did. You and me. The security division."

"But I'm not the security division anymore. I got busted back down to uniforms."

"That's what we want them to think."

I considered what Neptune said. It had the ring of truth and strategy to it.

"When I asked you what I should do after attacking those officers in the hallway, you set it up to get the senior officers alone in Council Chambers to determine my fate.

How do you know one of them is the murderer?"

"Tell me what you know about the murder."

"Are you ever going to answer one of my questions with an actual answer?"

"Yes."

"When?"

"Yes, I set it up to get those people alone in Council Chambers. Now tell me what you know about the murder."

"I don't know anything."

"Yes, you do. You found the body. Tell me about that."

Okaaaaaay. "I was excited about my job on the ship, so I got to the space station early. The first officers were given clearance and boarded before anybody else so they could check their assigned wards, but after them, it was board in order of arrival. I passed the security checkpoint and was one of the first crew members on the ship after the senior team. I went to my quarters and put my cases on top of the cabinet, and then I came here."

"Your cases?"

"My personal belongings. We were allowed to bring one trunk or two cases. I went with cases."

"Why?"

"One was filled with oxygen canisters, and I didn't

194

want to take a chance on anything happening to them."

"What was in the other?"

"Extra uniforms, Cat, and some Plunian potato chips."

"There are potato chips in the vending machines."

"Yes, but they're not Plunian."

"You're a potato chip snob?"

"I thought they'd be useful for bartering information or bribing anybody who found out my—the circumstances of my employment on the ship."

Up until now, I'd had the sense that Neptune knew of my records from the space academy and my family history. I should have been tossed off the ship the moment he learned the truth about me. But instead, he'd covered up my white lies about having been a last-minute replacement for Daila. I'd just accepted that because it was convenient for me, but now, I couldn't help think that if he had indeed accessed my records after I'd found the body in the uniform ward on that first day, he would have known I dropped out and that I hadn't taken Enemy Assessment.

If he were anybody else, I'd dismiss his incorrect notion as just that: not remembering the details from my file and assuming I'd finished out the curriculum to which I'd been assigned. Except this wasn't anybody else. This was Neptune. He'd already demonstrated a near-photographic memory, especially when it came to details related to my background. Details that I would have happily forked over my stash of Plunian potato chips to make him forget.

Understanding came over me, and pieces of information that meant nothing on their own but everything when combined settled into a picture in my mind. Neptune was the only person on this ship the captain didn't refer to by a title. When I'd asked him about that, he'd brushed me off. I doubted it had to do with him wanting to fit in or go unnoticed by the ship passengers. Anyone his height and build, dressed in fitted black clothes made from space fabric designed to hide the blood and ectoplasm of at least seventeen different known alien species (and a couple more that were only suspected to be in existence) wouldn't fade into the woodwork. Add in his dark pointed eyebrows, tawny skin, straight nose and strong chin, and anybody who wasn't afraid of him probably wanted to make a play for him.

No, Neptune didn't lack a title because he wanted to blend. He lacked a title because he'd done something to have it revoked. I wasn't sure how I was going to confirm my suspicion, but the more I thought about it, the more I knew I was right. It was the only explanation for why he didn't know I hadn't studied Enemy Assessment at the space academy.

"I need to get to the computer," I said. Before Neptune could argue the point, I continued. "Everybody out there thinks I'm the uniform lieutenant. If this place isn't in shape, they're going to report me for not doing my job."

"Why do you need the computer for that?"

"Inventory. I need to know which uniforms are here, what sizes, who has what. If anything was taken." I added an inspired thought. "The information could help you with the investigation."

He pulled a thin black tablet out of his bag and attached a keyboard, typed in a string of characters, and turned the computer to face me. "You're on the network."

I accessed the inventory management system and checked the pile of uniforms against what was on the manifest. It was a bogus job, made up to make me look industrious. It worked. Neptune appeared satisfied that I wasn't going to cause trouble and crossed the room to the other side.

I cloned the computer window and accessed an online news library. A few keywords later, I had the confirmation I needed.

It was Neptune who'd been tapped to teach Enemy

Assessment at the academy. He'd been the commander of the intergalactic space army. The same year I'd dropped out to move back to Plunia, he'd been let go from the academy and stripped of his title and credentials.

I didn't know what he'd done, but I would find out. It was the only course of action to finally let me know whose side he was on.

24: FOLLOWING ORDERS

I couldn't let Neptune know what I'd figured out. I used the excuse of removing my bubble helmet and placing it on the bench behind me to buy enough time to collect myself. The doors to the uniform ward opened, and Captain Swift came in. His bright red hair was reflected in the gold trim on his uniform.

"Lt. Stryker," he addressed me. "Good to see you at your station."

"It's my job to follow orders, Captain."

He nodded as if he agreed, but his expression looked conflicted. After a beat of silence, he turned to Neptune. "You're assisting Lt. Stryker in her duties?"

"I wanted to make sure she showed up to her post. Until she officially resumes management of the uniform ward, she's my responsibility."

Captain turned toward me. "Lt. Stryker, we all

appreciate your dedication to the ship. When we turn you over to M-13, I'll give you a commendation. It might make your transition easier."

I didn't know if the proper response to his offer was thank you or a different expression I'd heard from the language library that cataloged curse words from Earth. I chose to nod my head once in acknowledgment of his offer. He stared at me for a few seconds as if expecting more. When I said nothing, he turned back to Neptune.

"There's a problem with the hull."

"Engineering fixed that on day one."

Captain Swift looked at me. I pretended to be busy with the uniforms. The two of them stepped a few feet away so I couldn't hear. Well, shoot.

I continued to work while the captain and Neptune conversed. A problem with the hull? Again? I was rapidly losing faith in the Moon Unit 5 assembly crew. Or was "problem with the hull" a code phrase, like "the dog barks at midnight?" Were they just making an excuse to move out of earshot and talk about me?

I was a second lieutenant and should have been all but invisible on this whole journey, yet five days in I had two high-ranking officers in my ward and a tracking chip in the base of my skull. I continued pretending to sort uniforms. It didn't matter if I kept them organized or not.

I could fix whatever I did after the two men left. Right now, my attention was on them.

I opened the closet door wider and looked in the mirror on the inside. Neptune and Captain Swift's reflections were visible. Neptune was facing me, and the captain had his back to me. Neptune caught my eye and said something to the captain. They turned around and left.

Until I was dumped off on M-13, it was clear that my role in the room was to act as the uniform lieutenant, so that's what I did. I collected the soiled uniforms from the laundry chute. The uniform manager wasn't the most glamorous post on the ship, but for now, it was mine.

Each Moon Unit was equipped with a wall of dry cleaning devices. I pulled a garment screen out of its slot, attached the uniform to the screen by clips at the shoulder, cuff, and hem, and slid the screen into the narrow slot. Once I had all ten of the screens filled with uniforms, I sent a channel of sanitizing steam through the machines. I repeated the process two times, and then one by one removed the panels, unclipped the uniforms, and returned them to the inventory closet.

When the soiled uniforms were clean, I attacked the pile of uniforms that I'd dropped in the hallway. I sorted by size and color and then folded the uniforms neatly. A few had wrinkled badly while sitting in disarray, so I set them aside for pressing. I would not be responsible for Yeoman D'Nar catching anyone else on the ship in a wardrobe violation for improper uniform condition. If this was to be my station on the ship, then I was going to be the best darn uniform lieutenant they'd ever had. They would rue the day they questioned my commitment to my assignment.

The task was calming. For the first time since departure, I was doing work I could do in my sleep. I took my set of keys from the cabinet where I'd kept the BOP and unlocked the cage in the corner. The uniform press folded out, away from the wall. I inserted an energy charge into the base of it and switched it on. Seconds later the upper and lower panels of the press glowed neon orange. I slipped the first uniform onto the press and lowered the panels so they met, much like the press I'd rigged on Plunia to toast two sides of a sandwich at the same time. A thin stream of smoke trickled out and I opened it back up. The fabric of our uniforms was heat resistant. Some unexpected particle must have transferred onto a uniform, and I didn't want to ruin the press the first time I used it.

The uniform on the press was magenta like mine. I ran my fingertips across the surface, identifying a rough patch.

"Stryker." Neptune's voice tore my attention from the uniform. "You're to finish out your shift and then retire to your quarters. I'll have dinner brought to you. We'll reconvene tomorrow morning."

"Aren't you going to tell me what that was about?"

"It doesn't concern you."

"Why not? Because I'm a prisoner?"

"You're not a prisoner. You're a crew member."

"Yeah, right." I pulled the uniform off the press and tossed it onto the bench. "So, this is my life now. Sorting uniforms and keeping them wrinkle-free, at least until we land and then who knows? I guess when we're done I could get a job at a space laundromat. What with all of the sorting and pressing skills I will have perfected while on Moon Unit 5."

Neptune pressed his lips together like he wanted to say something but didn't. He left. I burned off a little of my anger by walking to the far end of the uniform ward and then back three times. The inactive alert on the uniform press beeped. I picked up the next wrinkled garment on my pile and fitted it onto the device. I repeated the process on autopilot for the rest of the uniforms on the wrinkled pile, ending with a neat stack of folded uniforms organized by size and color. The only one that sat by itself was the first one I'd pressed that had caused the press to sizzle.

I looked at the fabric more closely. Again, I had to run my fingertips over the surface of the uniform to identify the rough patch. The surface had cooled considerably, and the blob had hardened, making it easier to find. It was just above the insignia. I pulled an identification scanner out of the cabinet and positioned it on top of the hard spot, and then pressed my eye up against the lens and looked closely at the now-magnified section of fabric. With the ultraviolet light of the scanner illuminating the section in question, I made out a faint transfer of pearly blue now fused into the tight weave of the magenta heat resistant fabric.

I knew that pearly blue. It was the shade of nail polish worn by Yeoman D'Nar.

Yeoman D'Nar was a first officer. She'd been among the crew who'd boarded before I'd gotten clearance. She could have come to the uniform ward because it was part of her responsibility, but I had to wonder if she'd had a different reason to be in there before departure? Like killing the second navigation officer and sabotaging engineering herself?

25: SUSPICIONS GETTING CLEARER

Yeoman D'Nar had shown me no leniency from the moment we'd departed. I had assumed she was a tough boss, mistaking nastiness for management. The universe had long since accepted that female officers brought a different but valuable perspective to their positions of power, and training had equalized the techniques most leaders used. It would be generous to assume her nastiness had anything to do with her management style. It was probably inherent in her personality.

How unfortunate for her.

But what would be her reason for killing the second nav officer? Romance gone wrong? Or did she know something the rest of us didn't? Had he been the one to leak the poisonous gas into engineering and had she killed him to save us?

The day I found the body, I had asked Neptune who

the crew member was. Neptune had said the second nav officer's identity didn't matter, but I couldn't help wondering if it did. Protocol—confirmed by Doc Edison— prohibited us from treating him as anything other than his position on the ship. Neptune had enforced that more than others, but he'd been the one to tell me Lt. Dakkar's name. I didn't know if it mattered.

I went to the computer Neptune had connected for me and searched the network for crew member files. The name next to second navigation officer was D. Teron. It was clearly a mistake. Daila Teron was the original uniform lieutenant who I'd replaced.

But still, D'Nar's fingernail was evidence that she'd been here before me, and I wanted to know why. And until I did, I wasn't going to let her marred uniform out of my possession. The only problem was where to stash it? Yeoman D'Nar was my boss. She could search the uniform ward at any time. If I was correct and the pearly blue blob was from one of her fingernails, then she'd have to know she'd lost it. How long before she retraced her steps and ended up here?

I couldn't leave the uniform. And wandering the halls with it in my hand was flat-out suspicious. There *was* one way to get it back to my quarters without drawing attention to myself. I would wear it.

I glanced at the door. Neptune and Captain Swift had been gone for over an hour. My shift wouldn't be over for another two. Yet the longer I waited, the less sure I felt about taking the risk. If I waited too long, I'd talk myself out of it.

Reaching around the back of my black security uniform, I lowered the zipper as far as I could. I changed the position of my arms from up over my shoulders to underneath and unzipped the rest of the way. Ingrained modesty made me turn my back to the entrance even though I was alone. I leaned forward and shook my arms out of my sleeves, and then pushed the uniform off me to the floor. I stepped one foot out of it, and then the other, leaving it in a pile while I quickly stepped into D'Nar's. I heard the doors to the uniform ward open. I pulled the uniform up and looked to see who'd entered.

"Sylvia, oh, geez, I didn't know you were changing." Vaan's eyes went wide.

"Turn around!"

"Yes. Sorry." He faced the doors. "Do you need help with your zipper?" he asked over his shoulder.

"No," I said emphatically. I slipped my arms into the narrow sleeves—were D'Nar's arms really that thin?—and reached behind me to slide the zipper up. The narrowness of the sleeves made it difficult to bend my arms, but I made do. When I was fully dressed again, I picked my black security uniform off the ground and tossed it into the laundry bin.

"I'm done," I said.

Vaan turned around. His eyes took in the uniform on the press, the pressing device, and the neat stack of inventory on the bench behind me. Apparently satisfied that I wasn't up to something I shouldn't be, he didn't comment on my state of undress when he'd entered.

"I wanted to check on you," he said.

"Why? Because the head of Moon Unit security shot a tracking chip into me? Or because I was the subject of a meeting in Council Chambers? Or because I lost everything when the space pirates destroyed Plunia? No, it can't be that, because you're Plunian too and you don't seem to be upset. Or, oh. Maybe it's because you think I'm helpless and I need you to save me?" I tapped my finger against my cheek like I was considering those options. "I sure hope it isn't that one. I would have to be pretty delusional to think that you of all people would save me."

"Syl, that's not fair."

"No, Vaan, what's not fair is you finagling your way onto the ship in some misguided prince-who-saves-the-day act. You had your chance to do the stand-up thing for me once. Don't pretend you're trying to make up for past errors in judgment."

"You're way off base here."

"Am I? Because let's see. How many times have you done something that didn't advance your career?" I rolled my eyes up toward the ceiling and pretended to think. "I'm drawing a blank. Jump in if you got anything."

For the first time since Vaan had become a member of Federation Council, I saw him get angry. His eyes narrowed, his fists balled up, and his dark purple skin turned a deep shade of midnight violet. Acts of violence were completely verboten in Federation Council, and I knew he wouldn't risk his standing by acting out physically. But I was so mad myself that I stood my ground and stared back at him as intensely as he stared at me. The air felt prickly, like someone had turbocharged the atoms in a bath of electricity and sugar.

We stood like that, facing each other, with no words spoken, long enough for the inactive beep to initiate on the pressing device again. The sound startled me. I looked at the crumpled pile of fabric on the board and snapped out of my anger. I picked up another uniform, fitted it onto the board, and attacked the wrinkles.

My actions had a calming effect on Vaan as well. His coloring returned to normal. When it became impossible to ignore him, I looked up. I kept one hand on the iron, more for stability than because I planned to use it as a weapon.

"Sylvia, there's something bigger going on here than you know."

"There's nothing between us, Vaan. Not anymore."

"I'm not talking about us. I'm talking about Moon Unit 5."

"You've been on Moon Unit 5 for three days. I know more about this ship than you ever will."

"Listen to me. Please. This ship should never have been cleared for departure from the space station. I can't tell you anything more than that, but I need you to trust me."

"I can fight my own battles. I have for years."

"I don't want to see you become collateral damage in a battle that isn't yours."

I studied Vaan's face, looking for signs that he was manipulating me. All I saw was honesty.

I pulled the uniform off the board, shook it out, and then folded it. I'd hoped Vaan would take the hint from my resumed activity that I was moving on from our conversation and he should move on as well. He didn't. He stood in the same spot, watching as if waiting for me to complete my task so we could continue our conversation.

"What are you waiting for?" I asked. "I don't know what you said to convince the captain to make a secret, unscheduled stop at Federation Council and bring you on board the Moon Unit, or how the crew even managed that without everybody knowing we'd made a stop. But if that was meant to be some grand gesture to win me back, then forget it. You made your choices, and I made mine. I didn't ask you to show up unannounced on my ship. I was here first."

"You're wrong about so many things," Vaan said.

"Like what? Tell me one thing I've said that you know for a fact isn't true. Go ahead. I'm not dumb, Vaan. I know way more than you think."

"You're wrong about me convincing the captain to make a secret unscheduled stop to pick me up. I was the first person on board this ship. I boarded the ship before you, before the crew, before anybody."

"Were you here? In the uniform ward?"

"I was everywhere. Federation Council status gives me unrestricted access to every ward on the ship."

He turned around as if to leave, but stopped before activating the doors. "Change your uniform before

Yeoman D'Nar sees you. There's a stain above your insignia."

Our eyes connected for a long moment before he turned back toward the doors and left.

I hated to be wrong. As Pika would say, I hated it hated it hated it. But this time, being wrong had given me a valuable piece of information.

Vaan wasn't here for the reasons everybody thought. He was hiding something. And admitting to having been on the ship before anybody else meant I could add him to the list of suspects who could have committed murder.

26: MORE SUSPECTS

I finished my shift and headed to my quarters. It was easy enough to keep my head down and avoid talking to the other crew members. Between the assault in the hallway and any rumors that may have sprung up about me after the session in Council Chambers, I wasn't the most popular person on the ship. There'd been a time when I'd hoped to make friends on Moon Unit 5. Those days were over.

When I reached my quarters, I slipped out of D'Nar's uniform and into a robe. The only regulation uniform I had left was the one I'd torn the sleeves from on day one, and until I could retrieve a fresh uniform from the ward, I was going to have to repair this one or risk another infraction. I didn't know yet if Yeoman D'Nar had bigger reasons for riding my case since I arrived on the ship than just being mean, but until I knew if she was the murderer,

I wasn't going to give her an excuse to come after me. And if I *did* find out she was responsible for the death of Lt. Dakkar, my lack of regulation uniforms would be the least of my problems.

I got my sewing kit out of the bottom of my closet and sat at the table to work on the repairs. It would have been both faster and easier to do in the ship's workroom, but that would require me to leave my quarters, and I wasn't intent on making any public appearances.

As I lined up the edges of the fabric and started to sew, I thought over Vaan's words. If he'd been thinking clearly, he never would have admitted to having been on this ship before we departed. That meant someone expected trouble and applied for a representative early. Had Vaan volunteered for the assignment because of me? Hardly likely. Nobody on this ship knew I'd be here. So was it a coincidence? As a woman of science and reason, I hated coincidence. I liked when things fit into a pattern and made sense.

If Vaan wasn't here because of me, and his presence wasn't a coincidence, then I could see only two other options. Number one: someone had banished him to the ship in the hopes of getting rid of him. Number two: Vaan had arranged to be on the ship to commit murder.

Which meant I now had two solid suspects.

As my fingers nimbly handled the repairs to my uniform, it occurred to me that there would be a value to solving the murder on my own. In a conclusion that possibly only I would reach, it seemed that removing Moon Unit 5 from danger and saving a ship filled with vacationers who might tell their friends and even return for second and third trips would be worth, say, the price of my freedom. I had never heard of anyone successfully removing the chip from their spinal cords once implanted, but that didn't mean it couldn't be done. And if I was enough of a hero to save the luxury moon cruiser from bad press, then maybe I could even convince the owners to keep me on board.

Who was I kidding? There was no future for me with the Moon Unit corporation.

I finished repairing the second sleeve and stood up to change. I untied my robe and let it fall to the floor and then stepped into my uniform and bent down to lift it up. The doors opened.

"I hate those doors!" I said. I whirled around and found Neptune and Pika in the hallway. "A minute, please?"

Neptune grabbed Pika's skinny arm and pulled her a step backward. The doors shut.

After today, I was never going to take my uniform off

again! I finished dressing and opened the doors. Neptune and Pika still stood there. "My old uniform is in the uniform ward. You can get it there."

"That's not why we're here."

"Then what do you want?"

His eyes hovered some distance above my head. "Show her," he said.

Pika raised her eyes up to meet mine. She moved her hands from behind her and held out Cat.

I turned around and scanned my room. Because Cat's motion detectors were triggered by light, he occasionally walked around and fell off things. Sometimes I'd leave him on the bed and find him on the floor across the room. It added to the feeling that he was a live pet. But today, I'd been so distracted by Vaan and D'Nar that I hadn't looked for him when I got back after my shift.

"Where did you find him?" I asked. I reached out to take him and Pika pulled him away.

"Tell her," Neptune said.

Pika looked embarrassed. "I took him."

"Tell her everything."

"I took him, and I broke him." The pale pink alien girl held Cat toward me butt-first. The power panel above his right hind leg was open, and two wires jutted out. "I'm sorry."

I raised both eyebrows. Gremlons weren't known for their ability to feel sorrow or remorse. Pika's apology had been coerced and, judging from the way she quivered while she stood next to Neptune, I had a pretty good idea of who had been the coercer.

"It's okay. I built him, so I can fix him. Come on in and sit down." I looked up at Neptune's face. "I'll take care of her from here, thanks."

"We need to talk."

"Fine. Talk."

Neptune put his hand on my forearm and pulled me into the hallway. I looked up and down the hall to see if anyone had seen him manhandle me, but no luck.

"What do you think you're doing?" I said, but no sound came out of my mouth. "Great. This again. Where can I get one of those sound-cancelling thingies? You know, so I can sneak up on *you* and catch you naked."

Neptune glared at me like he'd heard what I'd said. He pointed to me, and then to him, and then at a door across the hall. I rolled my eyes but followed him inside. As soon as the doors swished shut behind us, he spoke.

"I need a favor."

"You have a lot of nerve. You think I'm going to do a favor for you?"

"I'm going on a mission. Solo. I need you to keep an

eye on Pika."

"Why? Why are you so protective of her? She could be behind everything. She's a stowaway."

"She's not a threat."

"How do you know that?"

"Can I count on you to look out for her?"

"Pika got onto this ship without anybody knowing and she's kept herself out of trouble better than I have. I'm pretty sure she can take care of herself until you get back."

Neptune's dark eyes bored into me. I stared back. Twenty-four hours ago, I might have told him what I'd figured out about Vaan and Yeoman D'Nar and everybody else, but not now. Too much had changed since them and Neptune was partly to blame.

I crossed my arms. "Pika knows where to find me if she needs anything."

"Good." He glanced down at my chest again.

"Is there a problem with my uniform?" I asked.

"No."

"Okay then. If you want to keep talking, look at my face."

"We're done."

"You can say that again."

I turned around and held my hand up. The doors

didn't open. I waved my hand back and forth over the flat red sensor mounted to the wall, but nothing happened. Neptune raised his open palm and the doors parted.

"Showoff," I said. I stormed across the hall. He didn't follow.

When I reentered my quarters, I found Cat sitting on the table. Pika was asleep in my bed. I changed into a silver jumpsuit made for lounging in the off hours. Like my blankets, the fabric adjusted to temperature but was also shot through with color-morphing threads. I set the dial to a soothing shade of amber and pulled my tools out of the closet.

My motivation for repairing Cat wasn't entirely because I wanted a distraction. When I'd built him, I'd inserted a small recording device. It only retained twenty-four hours of content because I hadn't seen a need for more, but now that I knew Cat had been with Pika, and for a portion of that time, Pika had been with Neptune, I wanted to know what they'd said.

Working with tools on a problem such as this had become second nature before I'd turned ten. My dad had been the first to notice how I'd take things apart and rebuild them. At first, it was a game to see if I could. Once I mastered the reassembly portion, I'd learned how to make things better. Soon the other kids on Plunia showed up with their broken toys and gadgets, and after that, it was their parents. I quickly learned my skills weren't common, and the families who treated my parents poorly quickly learned my repair work came with a price. I'd hidden the money from my parents because I didn't think they'd let me keep it. The longer I went without spending it, the more I knew once I did, it would be for something important.

I'd spent it all on a doctor willing to fake the results of my physical so I could work on Moon Unit 5. Look where that had gotten me.

I pulled on my magnification goggles and peered into the exposed power panel on Cat's tush. The problem was easily identifiable. The exposed wires needed to be looped around the recording circuits and then reconnected to the grounding screw. Piece of cake. I picked up the smallest of my tools and set to work. A few minutes later, Cat was back up on all fours. I closed the power panel on his rump and pressed the playback button on his recorder.

"There's a problem with the hull."

"Engineering fixed that on day one. I conducted an inspection myself." I would have recognized the voices even if I hadn't already overheard the beginning of the conversation. Neptune and Captain Swift. This was the conversation they'd started before leaving me alone in the uniform ward. Pika must have been there the whole time.

"I didn't do it!" Pika said, sitting up in my bed. She looked around the room like she expected to get into trouble.

"It's fine, Pika. Neptune isn't here."

"But I heard him!" She pulled the covers up to her chin.

"You heard Cat." I pointed to the robot animal on the table. "Were you in the uniform ward today? Somewhere near Neptune and Captain Swift?"

Her eyes widened, but she didn't answer.

"I already know you were. Cat recorded their conversation. You must have been close to them if Cat picked up their conversation."

"I lost him," she said. "We were playing in a room with screens and then the giant and the captain came in. I got scared and hid under the table, and when they weren't looking, I left."

"You didn't hear what they said?"

"No. Some. Yes."

I set Cat on the table and moved to the foot of the bed. "Pika, why are you so scared of Neptune? Did he hurt you?"

"No! But he told me if I talked about him, he'd drop me off at the nearest space station."

Apparently, I wasn't the only one on the ship that Neptune tried to control with his threats. Except now, I was pretty sure I had dirt that I could leverage against him.

"Listen to me," I said. I reached up and ran my fingertips over the base of my skull. "I'll take care of Neptune. He won't do to you what he did to me."

"He saved your life," she said.

"Is that what he told you? He didn't save my life, he marked me for life. He inserted a microchip into me. Now anywhere I go, I'll be identified as an intergalactic law-breaker. I can't hide. Whenever I pass a security checkpoint, the chip will trigger an alarm. Nobody will listen to anything I say. You don't get chipped by accident."

She moved her head from side to side, her eyes never leaving my face. "The giant shot you with an ice pellet. I saw him take the chips out of Doc Edison's gun and replace them with dry ice. He knew there was a chance somebody in that room would demand you got chipped but he didn't know who it would be. When Doc resisted, the ice pellet started to melt. If anybody had seen water drip from the muzzle of the chip gun, they would have known what the giant did. And if anybody else acted when Doc hesitated, you *would* have been chipped."

"Neptune didn't chip me?"

"No."

I touched the back of my neck again and felt the wound. "I don't get it. Neptune is security. He should be the one to follow orders. Why would he go against them?"

"He was trying to protect you."

"Why?"

"Because he likes you."

27: NOT CHIPPED

I kept my fingers on my neck. The wound I'd felt last night had healed over and the skin felt like my normal Plunian skin: smooth but tough, like latex stretched over my musculature and bones. It seemed Pika was telling the truth.

"The session in Council Chambers happened yesterday" I said. "This morning, you were here. You tied me to the bed. You said Neptune told you to watch me."

"You were maaaaad." Pika drew out the word. "The giant was afraid you'd hurt yourself."

"Pika, how do you know Neptune?"

Her eyes grew wide and her ears popped up. "I told you, I'm not allowed to say."

All yesterday I'd operated under the assumption that Neptune had chipped me. The anger, the secrets, the threats. And the new evidence I'd uncovered.

Neptune didn't know about that. He didn't know about D'Nar's melted fingernail or the truth about Vaan's presence on Moon Unit 5.

"I have to talk to him. He said he was going on a mission. Where is he, surveillance? Is he in The Space Bar? Go into the closet and hand me the aqua chiffon dress. I'll meet him there."

"He's outside."

"Outside where? There is no outside. We're in the middle of the galaxy."

She pointed to the wall of the ship and nodded. "He went out there."

"He can't go out there. He'll die."

"That's why he told you to watch me. He's not coming back." Pika's eyes grew double the size they'd been. A giant tear dropped onto her cheek and ran down her round pink face.

I put my hands on Pika's narrow shoulders and made her face me. "Are you telling me Neptune is planning to leave the confines of the ship?" She nodded. "Do you know why?" She nodded again. "You have to tell me."

"I can't. I'll get in trouble."

"You have to."

"No."

I'd forgotten how quickly a Gremlon could move.

Before I could stop her, she was at the door. The sudden motion caused them to open. I lost valuable chasing time maneuvering around the table. By the time I was out the door, she'd disappeared down the hallway.

I went back to my quarters and dropped into the chair. This had been the craziest week of my life and it wasn't over yet. An hour ago, I'd had a person to blame. As it turned out, that person had saved my life. Up was down. Black was white. My home planet had been destroyed. Everybody I knew was on this ship, and I couldn't trust any of them.

I sat up a little straighter when the reality of that thought hit me. There was one person who had risked his career to save my life, and if Pika was telling the truth, he was about to risk his own life next. If something— anything—happened to him, a killer would go free, and the ship still wouldn't be safe.

I had to find Neptune. If only Pika had told me more.

But something she'd said stayed with me. She was afraid she'd get in trouble for hiding. Hiding where? The where didn't matter as much as the why. Neptune already knew she was on the ship. She pretended to be scared of him, but she didn't hide from him. She'd been hiding from someone else. And she knew what Neptune was about to do.

I remembered the captain coming to the uniform ward and talking to Neptune. "There's a problem with the hull," he'd said. And I'd heard it repeated right here in my quarters because Cat had recorded it.

I put my magnification goggles back on and used the pointy end of my tool to trigger the playback mechanism on Cat. Static sounded, at first, and a shock coursed through the metal into my fingers. I dropped the tool, shook out my hand, and then picked it back up and tried again.

"There's a problem with the hull."

"Engineering fixed that on day one. I conducted an inspection myself."

"I'm not sure how it happened, but the atmospheric changes in the past twenty-four hours have slowly eroded the repair work. We've lost four drones trying to analyze the depth of the problem. You're going to have to go out there."

Neptune cursed. "How did you lose the drones?"

"Someone within our force field has been using a radio disruptor. The ship has to be fixed manually."

Static returned. I shifted the point of my tool on the playback button and a small spark flew out of Cat, followed by a tendril of thin smoke. I'd fried his motherboard and now the rest of the conversation was gone.

Short of searching the ship, I had no idea where I'd find Neptune. He could be in security quarters downstairs, or in the supply room, or having his last meal. For all I knew, he was already on his mission. I didn't have time to waste on the wrong lead. Focus, Sylvia. Remember emergency protocols.

Conservancy of tactics: In an emergency situation, the best action is the one that requires the least effort and most potential gain.

Translated: don't waste time looking for Neptune. Find a way to make Neptune find me.

I didn't change out of my lounging jumpsuit. Instead, I ran toward the uniform ward. The plan: find my old security uniform in the laundry bin. Activate the communication device in the insignia. Ask Neptune for his location.

It was a good plan. So good, that when I got there, I ran smack into Neptune.

Who was in his own state of undress.

"Whoa!" I said after bouncing off his bare torso. I turned my back to him and held my hand over my eyes. "Okay. Great. I found you. I guess we're even now."

"What are you doing here?"

"I found out what you're about to do. Don't ask me

how I know. I just do. And I know what you did to me. What you didn't do to me. I don't know why you did—didn't—do it, but I know."

"We can talk about that later."

"If you go outside this ship to examine the hull, there might not be a later," I said. My voice cracked, betraying the badass soldier I'd been hoping to channel.

Neptune's giant hand closed around my upper arm and he spun me around. He was in his trousers, but his chest was still bare. He looked down at me, his face serious. "Go back to your quarters, Stryker. You're not needed here."

"Stop being so stubborn! If there's an external problem with the ship, you need the best possible person to handle the difficulties that might come with fixing it. That's me, not you. Get over your whole 'I'm in charge' thing and deal with it."

Okay, there's my inner badass! Except I'd just volunteered for a suicide mission.

We glared at each other. Neptune may have won more of these sorts of face-off battles in his life, but before he won this one, there was something I had to say.

"Pika told me you saved my life."

He arched one eyebrow into a sharp point. Three creases appeared on his forehead, running a diagonal pattern downward toward the eyebrow that wasn't raised. He kept his eyebrow arched as if waiting for me to continue before determining whether he could relax his face.

"They were going to chip me and you saved me. I can't say I understand why, but I'm grateful and I'm sorry for what I said last night."

"You remember what you said?"

"Not really, but I know what I was thinking when I woke up, so I'm guessing some of that came out before I went to sleep."

His eyebrow relaxed. He picked up the black T-shirt that rested on top of the center console and pulled it on and then crossed his arms over his chest.

"Whatever you're about to do, it's not safe," I said.

"The security of the ship is at risk. That's my job."

"Last time I checked, it was my job too. You said it yourself: I'm part of the security team."

"I'm not sending you out there."

"Neptune, there are a lot of things you're better at than I am, but not this. The Plunian part of me has a higher tolerance for atmospheric changes in pressure. If I wear my helmet, I can regulate my oxygen." I dropped my chin and looked at the floor. What I was volunteering to do, what I was asking Neptune to let me do, was so much more than what I'd signed up for when I'd hacked into the computer and uploaded my files to the crew roster.

It didn't matter. When I'd boarded this ship, I'd had hope for the future and what this job could turn into for me. I'd wanted to cut ties with the people who judged me by my dad's corruption. I'd wanted to make my mother proud. I'd wanted to prove that a part Plunian/part earthling who was the daughter of a poor ice miner could make more of herself than anybody expected.

None of that mattered anymore. Everything I'd held dear was gone.

When I looked back at Neptune, he was still staring at me, but his expression had changed from judgment to assessment. If he were applying the principles I'd expected to learn from him at the academy, then he was weighing the odds of a successful mission with him outside the ship versus me. Of every single argument I could have made: youth, size, agility, girl power, it all came down to one thing.

"You have to let me do it. I have nothing left to lose."

28: NOTHING TO LOSE

Neptune walked to the locked cabinet mounted on the wall. He entered a ten-character code into the keypad and the cabinet opened. Inside were uniforms unlike any I'd seen on the ship. Thick, flame-retardant fabric with accordion-like pleats at the shoulders, elbows, hips, and knees. Orange reflectors were evenly spaced at ten-centimeter intervals. It was big enough to accommodate a separate uniform underneath.

Neptune pulled one from the top of the pile and handed it to me. "Put this on. It's insulated against temperature and pressure changes. I'll supply you with fresh oxygen canisters after you're suited up."

"Okay." I took the uniform from him and undid the zip closure. I put one foot into it. Neptune tapped my shoulder. When I turned around, he was holding the black security staff uniform I'd planned to retrieve. "Wear this underneath."

"Why?"

"I'll be able to hear you through the transmitter." He handed me the uniform. "I'll wait out front."

"Neptune." He stopped just before reaching the door. "No matter what happens tonight, you'll still have a problem. Someone wants to destroy Moon Unit 5, and they've already killed once to protect their identity. Focus on the murder and you'll catch them."

"Why do you say that?"

"It was the secondary crime. It was sloppy. I've been thinking about what I saw when I found the body, and I've come up with a list of suspects."

"We'll talk about this later."

"There might not be a later."

"You're coming back, Stryker." He raised his hand and the doors opened.

I needed to make him listen to me. I knew more than he did: about D'Nar's nail polish and Pika hiding in the uniform room and Vaan and my history. I knew Doc Edison had tanks of gas in Medi-Bay and could easily have smuggled carbon monoxide onto the ship. I knew Purser Frank lied about nitrous oxide at Happy Hour, Uma Tolst had access to the reserve of gas tanks as well, and Martians had baited me before I attacked them.

Neptune *had* to listen to me. I had to make him. I said the one thing I'd been holding back. "I know you were stripped of your title."

He froze. He turned his head slightly to the side. "Get into uniform. We'll finish this conversation in the repair chamber. I'll wait outside." He turned away from me and left.

I changed from my temperature-adjusting jumpsuit into my security uniform and pulled on the white space suit over it. The sleeves, hem, and neck of the suit had metal grooves that would lock onto my boots, gloves and bubble helmet. I secured my boots to the hems of the suit, picked up my bubble helmet and my gloves, and left the safety of the uniform ward behind me.

We walked in silence. It wasn't unlike the other times I'd walked with Neptune through the ship, except this time I wouldn't have minded some innocuous chatter. We took the elevator down to the security level where I'd spent time in the holding cell before proving myself a hero. I guess there were some things I was doomed to repeat.

The pressurized entrance to the repair chamber was on the wall behind the desk where Neptune had sat. He activated a number of buttons on the control panel and then flipped a large red switch on the wall. The dial behind him spun slowly. He grabbed one of the spokes, leveraged his body weight against the concrete wall with one of his boots, and pulled. For all the times I'd seen him flex his sizeable biceps, this time he did it out of necessity and not intimidation. He opened the round door and tipped his head.

"Get inside. We'll talk once we're secure."

I stepped into the chamber. Unlike the dinginess of the rest of the security level, the repair chamber was bright white, shiny, and pristine. A channel of air jetted past me into a vacuum, designed to keep anything from settling inside.

Neptune pulled the massive door shut behind him. He opened a flat, black computer and plugged a few attachments into the ports.

"Shouldn't you use that giant computer on the other side of the door?"

"Can't. This door blocks all signals. The only way for me to maintain a connection to the ship is through a radio signal."

"How exactly did you expect to do this by yourself?"

He looked at me for a moment, and then back at the screen. Apparently, I wouldn't be getting an answer.

"We're approaching a suspected wormhole. Normally we'd blast through it, but if the ship is damaged, the hull will deteriorate when we go into hyperdrive."

"Can't we wait until we reach Ganymede and inspect it there?"

"Depending on the damage, that might be too late."

"What are the risks of passing a wormhole at our current speed?"

"We could pick up an unwanted passenger. Or a contaminant. Or come to the attention of space pirates. The risks are numerous and unpredictable. The only thing we do know is that we need to maintain our current speed to examine the fracture in the ship and seal it. Once we're done, we have to resume our speed or risk attack. Are you clear on your assignment?"

I nodded. "How long do we have before we arrive at the coordinates?"

He looked at his watch. "Seventeen minutes."

"How much time will I have before we come out of that pocket of space?"

"Five minutes."

What neither of us said: in twenty-two minutes, we'd know if I was successful or if I—and subsequently the ship—were on our way to becoming space dust.

I secured my helmet onto the thick white uniform and then pulled on my gloves. Neptune buckled each of them. He removed two oxygen canisters from a black bag by his feet. One can lasted twelve hours. Two cans were more than enough. He pulled the pin in both and took a deep inhale from each of them. He was testing to make sure they hadn't been tampered with like the ones used to poison the engineering crew.

He nodded at me. I turned around and he secured each to the chambers that were molded into the uniform for that very purpose. He fed the hose into the opening in my helmet and tapped me on the shoulder. I took a deep breath of pure, cold oxygen. It reminded me of Plunia.

Tears formed in my eyes and I blinked several times to make them go away.

"You're coming back," Neptune said. No promises to rescue me if something went wrong. No proclamations of feelings left unsaid. Just three words: *you're coming back.* Said with such conviction that I believed him.

"Keep an eye on Vaan," I said. My voice was muffled by the helmet, but I could tell by Neptune's expression that he'd heard me clearly.

"He's Federation Council."

"He was on the ship before any of us. He's the youngest member of Federation Council and his loyalties could have been compromised."

Neptune's expression changed. "Who else do you suspect?"

"Yeoman D'Nar. Earlier today when I was pressing the uniforms, I found one with a melted pearly blue blob on it. I think it was one of her fingernails from the first day."

Talking about something other than my possibly impending death helped with my nerves.

"Doc Edison knows everything we know. He knew about my physical being faked and he looked the other way. That's a direct violation of the code of senior officers of a spaceship. He knew how the carbon monoxide would affect the crew, and he'd know how to tamper with one of my canisters. He was quick to get the second navigation officer out of my ward the day I found the body and he instructed me to report to him for a physical after my shift. If it hadn't been for my uniform infraction, he would have had a chance to poison me as well. Nobody would have questioned him if his report linked my death to the officer in the uniform ward."

"Who else?"

"Pika."

"What about Pika?"

"She's a Gremlon. They're notorious pranksters. I don't think she's capable of murder and sabotage, but she was in the uniform ward, and she told me she's a stowaway."

"It's not Pika."

"How do you know?"

"Pika is my—it's not Pika. You said five. Who else?"

"Well, if you're *sure* it's not Pika, then there's you."

"Me?" He seemed genuinely surprised, but not mad.

"When I look past your overwhelming charm," I paused to make my point, "I'm left with the fact that you showed up in the uniform ward even though my Code Blue hadn't been acknowledged. You had access to every part of the ship because of your security clearance. It would have been within your job description to take the second nav officer out if you thought he was a threat to Moon Unit 5."

"Not bad. Anything else?"

"You weren't in uniform, so you might have been trying to go unnoticed. And," I paused. "you don't have the proper credentials to hold the position you have on this ship."

"When you put it like that, I *do* sound guilty."

Lights on the computer panel activated. A timer was displayed. It was set for three hundred seconds.

"I better get into position," I said.

I climbed the rungs on the side of the repair chamber. A long, thick cord hung on the wall by the pressure-sealed escape hatch. I grabbed the end and hooked it onto the loop on the back of my uniform. It was small consolation to know that if something went wrong while I was outside the ship, my body could (possibly) be retrieved.

Nothing prepares you for the moment when you look out the window of a spaceship at the vastness of the universe and realize how inconsequential you are. As I waited for signs that the ship was slowing down, looking for the never-ending blackness to become recognizable as the nebulas, carbon particles, and shimmery space dust that I had previously only seen from the telescope at the space academy, I knew something was wrong.

We weren't slowing down. There would be no pocket of time and/or space for me to identify the problem with the hull and repair it—no five minutes. Not even five seconds. This whole mission was a trap.

I glanced down at the bottom of the chamber for Neptune. The heavy metal door was open and Neptune was gone.

29: SUICIDE MISSION

I was alone in the repair chamber. Neptune was missing and his computer was unattended. The red indicator light on the side of the computer blinked at twice the pace that it had when he'd first activated it. The timer display continued to count down the seconds until the hatch opened. When it did, I'd be sucked out of the ship by the force of the atmospheric pressure. I didn't know how much time I had, but I knew I didn't have much.

I jumped off the rungs and free-fell to the base of the chamber. The cord attached to my containment suit jerked me short of crashing into Neptune's computer. I flailed my arms around behind me to unhook the cord. Seconds after the metal disconnected and swung into the side of the chamber, the red blinking light turned bright blue.

Crap!

I grabbed the computer and jumped out of the repair chamber, slamming the heavy round door shut with the force of my weight against it. The mechanism locked into place. I didn't know what would happen on the other side of the door and I wasn't going to stick around to find out.

I tucked the computer under my arm and ran as fast as I could down the hallway toward the cell. After everything I'd learned about Neptune, after him arresting me and jailing me and freeing me and pretend-chipping me, I couldn't believe he'd betrayed me. He was a master at manipulation. I wondered if I would have seen his betrayal coming if he hadn't been banned from teaching and I'd been able to take his course.

Wait a minute. How did Neptune know we had five minutes in which to check the stability of the ship? How did he know about the problem with the ship in the first place? Engineering had been compromised. So where had he gotten the schematics, the timetables, and the intel reports? And how could he possibly have known I'd show up in the uniform ward after Pika told me how he'd disobeyed orders to keep the doc from chipping me in Council Chambers?

He couldn't. He'd shown up prepared to unlock a suit for himself. I hadn't even known what was in that cabinet, and that was my responsibility. Neptune had taken the information he'd been given and planned to conduct the repair mission himself.

And if Neptune had been inside the repair chamber when he entered the code to release the pressurized door, the atmospheric pull would have sucked him out into zero space right after me. We would have died within minutes of each other.

So, where had he gone? He'd left his computer. He'd left the indicator on. I'd trained for years for an emergency just like this one. It was do-or-die time. Time to prove if I were the person I'd always wanted to be.

When Neptune had me in lockup, I'd watched him work. His computer wasn't all that different from the training computer in my Level 3 courses. I dropped into his chair and ran my hands over the colorful knobs and switches and buttons. I pulled off my gloves and ran my fingers under the bottom of the desk. There was a small button on the right. Yes. That was what I'd been hoping to find.

Hostility among the ranks of ship personnel was rare but not unheard of. Those of us who made it through our classes on tactical advantages had the option of studying either computers or drone technology. I'd opted for computers. My partner, Zeke Champion, told me his dad was in charge of computer repairs on space fleet vessels.

One day, when Vaan stayed late to meet with political leaders, Zeke told me to crawl under the desk and look for a button. Surprised that he was right, I bribed him with Plunian potato chips until he told me what the button did. It blacked out the computer from the ship's operating system, forcing it to function without a connection to the network. It was called going dark. I'd asked him why anybody would want to do such a thing.

The answer was deceptively simple. When you didn't know who was tampering with your information, you went dark so nobody knew what you knew. It was the difference between RSVP'ing to a party and showing up on someone's doorstep unexpected. The hazards of such an action so far outweighed the benefits that I felt like I'd wasted a perfectly good batch of homemade Plunian potato chips as a bribe.

If I got out of this alive, I was going to find Zeke and cook him a five-course meal.

I pressed the button and the computer system went dark. A moment later, a flash of neon green burst through the middle of the screen. Small pixels of color broke away, leaving a small, spinning insignia.

Counter security network. Enter code word.

Ten white squares blinked on the screen. Ten letters. Neptune's code. I didn't know Neptune's code. I didn't know anything about Neptune. How was I supposed to figure this out?

I clawed at the thick white containment suit until it was in a pile on the floor. I bent my head down toward the transmitter. "Neptune, it's Stryker. I'm at your computer. I'm trying to access the counter security network and I need your code. Does this thing work two ways?" I slapped at the transmitter. "Neptune! Where are you!"

"Stryker," he said. "I'm in here."

His voice came not from the transmitter, but from the holding cell where I'd spent my first night. I approached the area when I saw him. He was on the ground. There was a large gash in his shirt and blood covered the fabric by his shoulder.

"Don't." He held up his hand. "Beams."

I stopped short right before the high-intensity light beams appeared. The floor to ceiling barrier caused sweat to run down the side of my head into the collar of my uniform. I slapped my palm against the button on the wall. The beams didn't retract.

"Why won't they turn off?"

"You need a top-level security card to deactivate them."

"You need Doc," I said. "I'll get him."

"Not Doc. Save the ship."

"I need your code."

He closed his eyes. His chest rose and fell with labored breathing. His lips parted and a word came out, faint and barely decipherable. "No."

Neptune's pain was evident. He was on the floor, his back up against the cot that I'd rested on four days ago when he'd treated me like a criminal. He kept his left hand on his shirt, pressing the fabric against the open wound. His eyes were half open. He was fading.

"Neptune!" I shouted. He opened his eyes. "Man up. What's your code?"

"Daila Teron."

30: FALLING TO PIECES

I stood, frozen on the ground outside of the cell. Had I heard Neptune correctly? Had he just said his code—the code to the dark security network—was Daila Teron? As in, the original uniform lieutenant who I'd hacked my information on top of to take her place on the very ship I was trying to save?

"Stryker."

The sound of my name snapped me out of it. I ran to the computer. The ten rectangles blinked at me. I activated the keyboard and pecked the letters out one by one. D-A-I-L-A-T-E-R-O-N.

Access granted.

I didn't have time to stop to think about the why of it all.

The first thing I did was run diagnostics on the ship. If there were truly a problem that required Neptune—or me, in my save-the-day gesture—to leave the safety of Moon Unit 5, armed only with two canisters of oxygen and an untested tether to a ship that was still moving through the galaxy so fast we'd disintegrate before blacking out, then I needed to know what it was.

The ship's systems were listed as Code Green. Totally normal. I set the timer to backtrack and show me the diagnostic logs for the past twenty-four hours.

All clear.

There was no threat. There had never been a threat. The emergency mission was a ruse to get us out of the way.

I closed the dark network and returned the computer to its normal state. Someone else had been down here long enough to attack Neptune. I didn't know when or how or why. I didn't know if they'd seen him on the computer in the repair chamber or me climbing the rungs to the hatch. I didn't have the time to stop and worry about it.

I stuffed the containment uniform underneath Neptune's computer and crept toward the cell.

"Stryker," Neptune said. His voice sounded weak. The hot beams of light cast a bluish glow over him, and the blood on his shirt looked purple, not red. He pulled his hand away from his chest and slid his space gun across the floor. It glided between the beams and hit my boot.

"Save yourself."

I picked up the gun and felt the heft of it in my hand. "Don't die on me, Neptune." He held my stare for a long, tense moment. There wasn't time for anything more.

I ran to the elevator. The doors swished open and I jumped in, sidestepping something blue on the floor. It was a uniform—a medical uniform. One band on the sleeve. Medical ward, first officer.

Doc.

My heart raced as the elevator sped to the floor with the uniform ward. The doors opened and I scanned the hallway. At the far end, Beryn and his green Martian cronies stood in a group. I raced toward them. When they spotted me, the group collectively backed away.

Beryn took the position in front of the rest of them with his arms held up. "Get away from us. We pose no threat to you." His eyes moved between my face and the space gun, and then back to my face.

I dropped the gun to my side. "Neptune is in the holding cell in security. He's injured. Get help."

"You're a uniform lieutenant. You don't give us orders."

Captain Swift joined us from the other side of the hallway. "But I do," he said. He pulled his radio from his side and spoke into it. "Emergency in the sub-basement. Officer down." He looked at me. "Is it bad?"

"Yes."

Captain Swift turned to Beryn and the others. "Disperse throughout the ship. Be on alert for intruders, stowaways, and anyone acting suspiciously. Code Red." He turned toward me. "Do you know who's responsible?"

I thought I did, but so much depended on me being right and I didn't want to screw this up. "No," I said tentatively.

"Captain," Beryn interjected, "the passengers. How will we know who's supposed to be here and who isn't?"

"Call Purser Frank," I said. "He'll know."

Captain Swift nodded once. The little green men scattered into the hallways. I went the opposite direction toward the uniform ward. It was the closest place I could think of where I could activate the emergency alarm to warn everyone on the ship.

In the uniform ward, I ran straight for the console and the button to communicate with the bridge. The cover was stuck. I set down Neptune's gun and clawed at the plastic bubble. The gun fell off the console. The bubble didn't budge.

I turned around, looking for something to use to smash it. My eyes rested on the iron I'd used to press the closet of uniforms earlier that day. It was too far away. I grabbed the makeshift BOP that I'd hidden in the center console, whirled around, face to face with the captain.

"Lt. Stryker," he said. "We have to get you to safety."

"I have to notify the bridge."

"I already did. You're in danger. Come with me," he commanded. He was calm. Stoic. In control, like a captain should be. He moved toward me and I willed myself to stand still. "Neptune will be fine. Doc Edison will see to that. Neptune went on a risky mission, and something must have gone wrong."

"Not Doc," I said. "He's—" I stopped. Something wasn't right. For the first time since being on the ship, Captain Swift was disheveled. His uniform jacket was wrinkled and the bottom closures weren't closed properly.

No. Not Captain Swift. Please, no.

I clung to the BOP with both hands, wishing there was a way to trade it for Neptune's gun. Gone was the rational side of me that defaulted to the knowledge I'd learned at the space academy. I was panicking. Nothing felt right.

But I knew. Captain Swift must have stolen a Medical uniform to frame Doc when he attacked Neptune. He'd discarded it in the elevator. He hadn't known I was in the repair hatch at the time.

There was no way to unknow what I'd figured out.

"You sent Neptune to repair the exterior of the ship," I said slowly.

Captain Swift stopped a few feet in front of me. "You

know about the mission?"

"You came here to the uniform ward to talk to Neptune about it. I overheard your conversation."

"Then you know what Neptune knows."

He said it slowly. Too slowly. My instinct was to answer quickly, in the manner expected of a subordinate officer in private conference with the captain. But he wasn't looking for a yes or a no. He was reading me to see *how much* I knew.

If I knew he killed the second navigation officer, leaked CO into engineering, and invented a fake mission designed to send Neptune to his death.

Yes, I knew. I didn't know why he'd done any of it, but in that moment, I was sure he was behind everything.

"You're a criminal. You sabotaged the ship and risked the lives of everybody on board. What I don't know is why. Maybe why doesn't matter." I stepped backward to put space between us.

"You know all that? I'm impressed. Here I thought approving the faked application of a low-income Plunian would be a safe move. Far safer than letting Neptune's protégé on the ship. She would never have accepted that her brother's death was an accident."

"Her brother?"

"Dakkar Teron, the second navigation officer."

My mind raced. I'd hacked my credentials into the

computer on top of Daila's credentials. The position of uniform lieutenant was minor enough that I'd assumed approval would be conducted by automated computer systems, or that someone would click a box and upload my files to the crew manifests. I hadn't expected my files to be reviewed by the captain himself.

"I can tell from your expression you're surprised. Did you think I was going to let a wild card onto my ship and potentially ruin my plans?"

"What do you need with a Moon Unit?"

"I don't need the ship. I need the *passengers* on the ship. The space pirates waiting for me at the destination point on Ganymede are looking for slaves. Worker bees. They're willing to pay top dollar."

"You're selling the passengers and the crew into slavery to space pirates?"

"Not the crew," he said. "They'll die in an unfortunate explosion shortly after the passengers disembark." He picked up one of the loose canisters of oxygen that had rolled across the floor. "These Moon Units. They sure are unlucky."

As we spoke, he'd crept toward me and I'd crept back. There was only so much room left in the uniform ward, and once my back was up against a wall, I'd have nowhere to go. I took another backward step past the console. My eyes cut to the plastic bubble over the button.

"Funny thing, you reporting a Code Blue on your first day," Captain Swift said. "Your CV didn't indicate you had any knowledge of our BOP. I couldn't take the risk of you being allowed to act on your own a second time." He knocked on the plastic bubble covering the red button. "Welded into place by Yeoman D'Nar. Following instructions to keep you from manufacturing reports of any other crimes."

"The crime I reported was real."

"Yes. But what are the odds that there would be two emergencies coming from the uniform ward? Yeoman D'Nar already thinks you're a nuisance. She might not even be all that upset when the chip in your head malfunctions and kills you."

The chip in my head. There was no chip in my head. I knew it. Neptune knew it. Pika knew it. But nobody else knew it.

Captain Swift thought he could take me out by short-circuiting a non-existent chip. He raised his space gun and spun one of the knobs on the top, and then pointed it at my temperature-adjusting lounging uniform that I'd discarded in a pile on the floor when I'd changed. He fired. A white beam shot out from the gun, and the garment glowed like it had been plugged into a power socket. Seconds later, the supposedly indestructible fabric was a mound of hardened mass, melted into a useless paperweight.

There might not be a chip in the back of my head, but I wasn't out of the woods yet.

I needed a weapon. I had nothing but a dogeared BOP. Neptune's gun sat on the console by the alarm button I couldn't activate. The iron was on the pressing board on the other side of the ship. Captain Swift had kicked the loose canisters of oxygen behind him, where they'd rolled up against the wall. It was him, me, and a pile of newly pressed and folded uniforms.

He raised his gun. "Maybe I should include you with my drop off to the pirates. Like a bonus. I bet a part-Plunian, part-earthling slave would earn me a little something extra." His eyes trailed down from my face to my torso, lingering in a way that told me exactly what kind of extra he hoped to get.

My stomach turned. I'd backed up so far that there was no place left to go. The bench with the folded uniforms jutted into the back of my legs. But somewhere in my brain, risk assessment told me the captain wasn't going to use the gun on me. Not if he expected to turn me over to the space pirates. I'd be of more value to him—and them—alive than dead.

"It's over, Lt. Stryker. Look on the bright side. You probably have a long, exciting life ahead of you. That's what you wanted when you left your planet behind, right?"

Whatever I'd wanted when I left Plunia was gone. Dreams, hopes, desires, goals. Destroyed by one man, one ship, one experience. Which was worse: that the man who'd granted my dreams was corrupt to the core, or that he'd only granted them because he'd expected nothing of me?

Anger built up inside me, ten times stronger than what I'd felt before attacking the Martians in the hallway. My skin turned neon purple. Captain Swift's eyes widened. I dropped the BOP and lunged. The attack took him by surprise and we fell. I got on my hands and knees and crawled toward the exit. He grabbed my ankles and yanked me backward. I clawed at the ground and kicked at him.

"You killed my mother!" I cried.

He wrapped his arms around my legs, restricting my movement. "You were supposed to be a cipher," he said between panting breaths. "A zero. A farmer's daughter with a dad in jail. Couldn't even pass the physical requirements to be on this ship." He bound my legs with a pair of crew trousers. "Why'd you try so hard, Stryker? Nobody cares. Especially now. Not your mother—she's dead. I made sure the pirates saw to that when they destroyed Plunia. And not anybody else who lived on your pathetic planet, unless that explosion blew them so far into the atmosphere that they caught up with the ship. Nobody will miss you when you're gone."

I spread my arms wide, grasping for a weapon. My fingers connected with my bubble helmet. I grabbed it in my right hand and rolled myself over, swinging it toward Captain Swift's head as hard as I could.

The fiberglass bubble connected with his skull. His eyes rolled up into his head and he fell to the side, his upper body draped across my legs. I was pinned.

His gun had fallen from his fingers. I twisted and strained to reach it. I could end this. Now. I was less than an inch away from the gun when the doors opened and Vaan entered. His foot connected with the gun and knocked it close enough to grab.

My hand wrapped around the grip and I aimed at the captain.

"Don't do it, Syl," Vaan said. "Don't throw away your future. If you shoot him, I can't look the other way."

"He's a criminal. He killed one crew member and poisoned two others. He had pirates destroy Plunia. He needs to die."

"That's not your decision," Vaan said. "Let Federation Council decide his fate."

I kept the gun trained on Captain Swift. Vaan secured the captain's wrists behind his back with council cuffs and shifted his body off my legs.

"Give me the gun," Vaan said. He held out his hand, palm side up.

I looked at Captain Swift, slumped on the ground, unconscious from my strike to his head. I looked up at Vaan's face, filled with forgiveness for a crime I hadn't committed.

The doors opened again, and this time Neptune came in. His shirt was torn away from his chest and a makeshift bandage was on his shoulder. Blood had seeped into it. He looked at me, and I saw in his expression everything I felt.

Neptune didn't have a title. He didn't have security clearance. He belonged on this ship about as much as I did. But he was here to do a job, just like me. And the reality of that job was nothing like he'd expected.

He aimed his gun at the captain. Fired. Once. Twice. The captain's body flinched with the first impact but not the second.

Captain Swift was dead.

Vaan spoke. "I have to report your actions."

"Do your job. I just did mine." Neptune handed the gun to Vaan. "Stryker is innocent of any accusations. Get her to Medi-bay." He left without looking back.

31: POST MORTEM

Moon Unit 5 arrived at Ganymede after all.

No damage had been sustained to the ship under the Captain's crooked direction, but the same couldn't be said for the crew. Dakkar Teron, the second navigation officer and brother of the original uniform lieutenant, had been murdered. Two members of the engineering crew had been poisoned with noxious gas. And Neptune was still recovering from the stab wound the captain inflicted when Neptune left the repair chamber to investigate a hunch that something wasn't right. Doc said Neptune would recover in time. Despite the way he grumbled about it, I knew he'd been just as thankful as the rest of us for the role Neptune played in protecting the ship and its passengers.

That included me. Sure, I'd figured out something

wasn't right when I looked out the porthole of the repair chamber and saw the speed at which we were moving. But Neptune had figured it out before then. He'd placed the outer seal of the repair chamber on lockdown, protected by his private log-in credentials. Even if I'd tried to open the chamber myself when I saw he was gone, I wouldn't have been able to. He'd made sure I wouldn't die before he went after the person who'd stabbed him and left him in the cell to die.

It was hard to be mad at him after that, but I managed. Mostly because I'd figured something else out too.

I stood by the ship's exit, saying goodbye to passengers heading out for a day of sightseeing. Since Plunia was now gone, Moon Unit Corporation had arranged for a space taxi to transport me, and all other crew members who had lost their homes thanks to the space pirates, from Ganymede to temporary housing on Federation Council property.

I was surprised by the number of people on the ship who said goodbye to me by name. Even Yeoman D'Nar had a few kind words, despite my accusations of murder based on the fake fingernail fragment I'd found in the uniform closet. It turned out D'Nar and Dakkar Teron, the second navigational officer, *had* tussled in the uniform ward before the ship departed, just not the sort of tussling I'd assumed. Her attitude problem was simply a defense mechanism to hide the fact that her lover had been found dead. When she realized she'd lost a fingernail, she feared incrimination.

I waited at the exit for Neptune. We hadn't spoken since the night he'd killed the captain. I didn't know if he thought I was a hero or a hindrance. I didn't know if he would have shot the captain if not for me.

He was among the last crew members to exit the ship. "Stryker," he said.

"Neptune."

He stood next to me with a black duffel bag over his non-injured shoulder. He hooked his thumb under the strap and hitched the bag up. "Take care."

"That's it? 'take care?' We never talked about what happened."

"Security crew doesn't talk about missions."

"Yeah, well, I'll never get a chance to work another cruise ship like this one. On paper, the only thing I'm qualified to do is farm ice, and now that Plunia is gone, the only ice farms are on Mars. I don't want to live on Mars."

"You got a place to stay?"

"That's not the point."

"I know." He looked off in the distance, past a row of space taxis. "Do you know why I took this job?"

"The chance to show off your sparkling personality?"

He smiled. "I made a mistake. Back when I had an

261

opportunity to teach at the space academy. I made a mistake and it cost me my credentials, my title, and my reputation. I cut myself off from everybody I knew. A friend I'd lost touch with contacted me about this job. We were at the academy together. It wasn't what I would have chosen if I'd had a choice. I was a soldier. Moon Unit Cruise Ship Security?" He shook his head to show how he felt about the choice. "Gotta set aside a lot of ego to go from protecting federation ships to babysitting a vacation vessel."

"You wanted a paycheck."

"I wanted to feel important again." Neptune looked away from the crowds and directly at me. "Thaddeus Swift was that friend."

There was no quick retort for that. I'd been so busy thinking about the losses I'd experienced while on Moon Unit 5 that I hadn't considered how Neptune's actions affected himself. He'd shot and killed the man who had pulled him out of his self-imposed exile. We had both made sacrifices. We would forever be changed by what happened. I'd dealt with loss when my dad had been arrested. I suspected this wasn't a first for Neptune either.

"Stryker, take it from me. It's not easy to lose the life you know. It's tempting to self-destruct. Some people withdraw. Others seek familiarity." Neptune's honesty was both surprising and welcome, but he wasn't getting off that easily.

"There never was a problem with the ship's hull, was there?"

"Captain Swift told me Engineering reported a crack in the exterior to him prior to departure. I ran a pre-flight inspection and didn't see any signs of maintenance or repair. Raised a red flag. I told him the problem was fixed, but I was on alert."

"You used me," I said. He raised one eyebrow into a sharp peak. "You suspected something was wrong as far back as the day you arrested me for being on the ship. You suspected Captain Swift and you used me as bait to get your proof."

"It's security's job to take risks to protect everybody else. You should know that. You attended the space academy."

"My dad got arrested and I had to drop out to help my mom on the ice farm. I thought you knew all that."

"My tenure at the academy ended before your dad was arrested. I assumed you graduated like your CV said."

I'd said a lot of stuff to Neptune since boarding the ship. I'd lobbied accusations at him. Insults. Sarcasm. Lies. And after all that, after having lived through what I had, knowing how unclear my future was, I felt I had little to lose from plain old candor.

"After I returned to Plunia, I hacked into the academy computer and downloaded the curriculum. I bought class lessons and used materials and taught myself as best as I could. If you checked up on me, you would have known my CV was bogus."

"Your credentials were bogus, but your knowledge was real. Nobody would deny that." We both turned to watch the crew of Martians deboard the ship. "Not even them."

"Can I ask you a personal question?"

Neptune raised his eyebrow again.

"What happened at the academy to make you leave?"

"I got involved with a student." He was silent for a beat. "Her name was Daila Teron."

Oh.

"You saw her name on the crew manifest. You expected her to be on the ship instead of me. Is that why you came to the uniform ward before my Code Blue was acknowledged?"

He nodded. "I wanted to establish some guidelines so there wouldn't be any conflicts of interest on the moon trek."

Neither one of us mentioned how poorly that had turned out for him.

I looked down at my magenta uniform. It was the same one I'd worn when I'd arrived. Over the past six days, it had been torn apart and put back together. It was the uniform equivalent to my life. And the longer Neptune let my statement go unanswered, the more I got the picture. "You knew from the first day you saw me on the ship that I didn't belong."

"Your presence on the ship raised some questions, yes."

I smiled to myself. "Is she coming to pick you up?"

"No. Daila and I were short-lived."

"But your password—"

"The last time I got involved with a subordinate, it cost me my job and my reputation. Using her name as a password was a reminder not to let that happen again."

"Is that a habit of yours? Getting involved with subordinates?"

"No."

The word hung in the air. With it came questions, answers, and unexpected emotions. Whatever I wanted to say was silenced by the sight of Vaan waving at me from the end of the docking station.

While Vaan and Neptune had maintained cordiality for the duration of the moon trek, there'd been no love lost between them. Vaan had initiated proceedings to strip Neptune of his rank and title. Nobody had told Vaan that Neptune had lost his credentials long before the moon trek had started. Including me. When the council came back with the ruling that no action would be taken against Neptune, Vaan's reputation took a hit. Put simply: the two men would never be buddies.

Pika skipped out from the ship. She held a large purple oxygen pop in one hand, and traces of the violet hue had smeared around the outside of her mouth in a ring. She skidded to a halt when she saw me talking to Neptune and tried to hide the oxygen pop behind her back. "Am I in trouble?" she asked Neptune.

"No. Just"—Neptune looked slightly embarrassed—"wait for me over there."

"Okay," She looked guilty for a moment, and then gave me one of her fifty-tooth smiles. "I'm glad you didn't die!" She hugged me, and then, in a flash, was at the end of the platform with the other departing passengers.

"What's going to happen to Pika?" I asked.

"She'll be fine."

"But she was a stowaway. I think the ship was her home."

"She lives with me."

"You—and Pika?" The thought surprised me. Pika had shown an odd loyalty to Neptune even though she was afraid of him.

"She left Colony 7 and bummed around the galaxy. I found her living on my property a couple of months ago. Didn't see the point in scaring her away."

"You let her on the ship."

"She followed me to the space station and snuck on board. That made her my responsibility."

"Security protocol demands that Federation Council be notified of stowaways aboard a passenger-bearing vessel. Based on Dakkar Teron's death, they would have instructed you to make a stop at the nearest space station and turn her over to their custody."

"Pika wasn't a threat."

"You wanted to take care of her."

"I didn't want to leave her to fend for herself."

"You're not so tough after all." I grinned at him.

Neptune's face softened. He looked out at the sky. It was lavender, a shade not too far from my part Plunian flesh. The sun, in contrast, was a small yellow circle over five hundred million miles away. As I absorbed the beauty of the galaxy, I had a hard time believing in the threat of space pirates and fighting amongst planets, of dry ice shortages and intergalactic wars.

"What's next for you?" Neptune asked.

"I'm going to live at the space academy and get my degree."

"There's a position for you here if you want it."

I turned to him, surprised. "Where? The moon trek is over."

"There will be more moon treks."

"You know the only way I got onto this ship was because I lied about my credentials."

"You're more qualified than any candidates I ever met. The corporation is launching Moon Unit 6 soon. Bigger ship, longer trek, more demanding passengers."

Before I had a chance to answer, he continued. "Think about it before you turn it down," Neptune said. He didn't look at me. "We make a good team, Stryker. Moon Unit Corporation would be lucky to have you."

I studied Neptune's profile: his intimidating stance, his arched eyebrows, his inherent toughness. And then I turned and looked the other direction at Vaan. Member of Federation Council. Part of the law and order of the galaxy. Plunian, like me. The men represented two different avenues: one to my future and one to my past. The decision was easier than expected.

"What's the range on that micro-transmitter in my security uniform?"

Neptune looked from the sky to me. "Why do you ask?"

"You'll need a way to reach me when Moon Unit 6 is ready to go."

He grinned. "See you soon, Stryker."

ABOUT THE AUTHOR

After two decades working for a top luxury retailer, Diane Vallere traded fashion accessories for accessories to murder. She started her own detective agency at age ten and has maintained a passion for shoes, clues, and clothes ever since.

Sign up for The Weekly DiVa for book talk, girl talk, and life talk. Get insider stories, first notice of contests, give input toward books in progress, and have fun: dianevallere.com/The-Weekly-Diva

SERIES BY DIANE VALLERE

Sylvia Stryker Space Case Mysteries

Samantha Kidd Style and Error Mysteries

Madison Night Mad for Mod Mysteries

Margo Tamblyn Costume Shop Mysteries

Polyester Monroe Material Witness Mysteries

CPSIA information can be obtained
at www.ICGtesting.com
Printed in the USA
LVHW021433281218
602058LV00001B/30/P

9 781939 197542